6th Grade
Dance
Contest

Darci stayed there gazing up at the poster for a minute. A dance contest. That sounded like so much fun. She'd gone to dancing class last year at the Y for a while. But wait a minute. She'd have to have a partner. She'd need to know a boy who liked her and liked dancing—a nice boy who didn't play tricks on her and laugh at her.

How could she get to know a boy? It was so much easier when you had friends. Then you could all get together and call boys on the phone. Or one of your friends might ask a boy if he liked you and help you that way. No way she could hope to do all that in a few weeks. But it was hard to get the thought of the dance contest out of her mind.

Darci and the *Dance Contest*

Martha Tolles

AN
APPLE
PAPERBACK

SCHOLASTIC INC.
New York Toronto London Auckland Sydney

No character in this book is intended to represent any actual person; all the incidents of the story are entirely fictional in nature.

ISBN 0-590-33824-2

12 11 10 9 8 7 6 5 4 3 2 1   7 8 9/8 0 1 2/9

Printed in the U.S.A.   11

First Scholastic printing, June 1987

to my husband,
my favorite dancing partner

Contents

Sitting With the Boys

Darci Daniels stepped up onto the school bus and looked at all the new, unfamiliar faces. Where would she sit? There wasn't a single empty seat, except in the back, where a lot of the boys were sitting and laughing and yelling at each other.

Darci stood in the aisle for a minute. Could this really be happening to her? Was she really on a new school bus, headed for a new school, thousands of miles away from her old school and old friends way back in California?

She started down the aisle trying to find an empty place. She'd worn her light blue jeans with her light blue sweater this morning and hoped she looked okay, like someone the other kids would want to get to know.

1

"Sit down," the bus driver yelled at her as the bus lurched around a corner.

Darci saw two girls who'd been in her class yesterday. Maybe they'd move over and make room for her; she headed toward them. But they were busy talking and didn't even glance up.

Darci hovered beside them for a minute. What do you say when you are brand-new and don't know anybody? She'd never been new before, so she wasn't really sure. But she guessed she'd better say something, otherwise she'd have to go on back to where all the boys were sitting.

"Hi," she blurted out to the two girls.

They glanced up at her with startled faces.

"Uh, hi," one of them said, still looking surprised.

"I'm in your class at school," Darci said.

"Oh, yeah. You're new," the same one said.

"Find a seat back there," the bus driver called out again.

The two girls didn't slide over, so Darci guessed she'd have to keep moving. She headed toward the rear of the bus. She'd have to sit with the boys. She wished one of her brothers were on the bus, at least, but they went to different schools.

The boys were all laughing and yelling about something or other. One of them, the one with the wild, curly black hair, was a boy who lived on her street. Nathan was his name. Well, she'd just ignore them, she told herself as she headed for the empty seat. She wished some nice friendly girl were sitting in the other half of it. But instead there was an older boy reading a copy of *Mad* magazine. This new school, Oakwood Middle School, went up to eighth grade. Her school in California stopped at sixth, so she'd been in the highest class. She wasn't used to going to school with these older kids.

Darci bent over to put her lunch bag and books on the floor. With a sigh, she eased into her seat. But wait a minute! What was that under her? Something soft and squashy went *squish, squish!* Suddenly, Darci felt something soaking right through her jeans to her skin.

She leaped up. "What's that?" she exclaimed. But it was too late because there, right on her seat, was a smashed, dripping-wet water balloon and a puddle of water!

"Ha-ha-ha, ho-ho!" All the boys around her rocked with laughter.

"Why you . . . you creeps, you!" She felt hot and angry and embarrassed. Wet jeans! Who needed wet jeans? How it would show on light blue! Of all days, why had she chosen to wear this pair?

"Why did you do that to me?" Darci demanded. To make matters worse, Darci felt her lips tremble. Which one of these creepy guys—?

"Hey, I'm sorry, Darci." That was Nathan, the one with the curly black hair and black eyes. He was sitting in the seat right behind where she had sat down. He spread out his hands and scrunched down in his seat, trying to look innocent. "I didn't know it was going to break like that. No kidding. Besides, I thought you'd see it or something."

"Oh, sure, I'll bet. And now what am I going to do?" No way could she get off this bus and go home.

"Look, it'll dry pretty soon." Nathan leaned over the back of the seat and took away the dripping, burst balloon.

"In about three hours," Darci said indignantly. She took out a few Kleenexes and mopped the seat. Then she turned around and sat down. She hunched forward, letting her hair slide over her face. She felt this annoying stinging in her eyes. What could she do? Her second day of school. Yesterday Mom had driven her to school be-

3

cause they'd had to see the principal. But today she was on her own.

She heard the boys snickering behind her. Back home, some of the boys had been cute and nice, but here . . . She stared out the window as the bus rumbled along toward Oakwood Middle School. Everything looked so different. It was such a cloudy, gray day—not like California, where it was usually bright and sunny. And now the bus was turning into the parking lot of Oakwood Middle School and there it was, a big, forbidding-looking red-brick building, nothing like her old one-story stucco school with its open walkways and patios.

The bus groaned to a stop, and everyone began to crowd out into the aisles. Darci picked up her books and lunch bag and refused to look back at the boys behind her as she pushed her way forward. She tried not to hear their laughs. They must be staring at her wet jeans. If there were only some way she could hold her lunch bag or her books behind her, or if only she had a jacket to tie around her waist.

Darci got off the bus as fast as she could. All she wanted now was to get to her classroom and into her chair and stay there until she was dry. But as she hurried across the parking lot, three girls caught up with her and passed her, giggling over their shoulders at her as they went by. Then two boys ran past her.

"Hey, what'd you do, wet your pants or something?" One of them leered at her. The whole world could see the wet spot, of course. Light blue would show anything.

"No way," she said loudly. All these kids surged past her, laughing, talking. Darci felt a stab of loneliness. If only she were with her old friends back home now.

She entered the school building and started down

the hall. Suddenly she heard another voice behind her.

"Well, what in the world happened to you?" She turned to see a girl who was in her class. Darci remembered the girl's name was Lisa. She was with a bunch of other girls. They all had superior smiles on their faces as if they thought something was just so funny. "Did you have—uh—an accident?" Lisa asked.

"You could call it that," Darci said. "Some nerd put a water balloon under me on the bus." All four girls laughed loudly. Darci tried to smile. "Maybe I should carry a sign around that says I SAT ON A WATER BALLOON."

"Yeah, yeah, you should," the one named Lisa agreed. Her blue green eyes looked very amused. "Who did it anyway?"

"Some boy named Nathan," Darci said.

"Nathan!" Lisa exclaimed and exchanged looks with the others. "Do you know him?"

Darci shrugged. "I suppose. He lives on my street."

"Really?" Lisa's eyes gleamed. "You ought to think of some way to get back at him. I wouldn't let him get away with that if I were you." She looked knowingly toward her friends.

"Yes," they echoed. "You should."

"I wouldn't mind," Darci agreed. But what could she do?

"So you're from California?" Lisa went on. The teacher had told the class that yesterday.

Darci turned to keep her backside to the wall. "That's right. It's a great place." She wanted to tell them just how great it was, but she didn't think she should.

"I suppose you have a lot of good horses out West there?" one of the other girls asked.

"Uh, sure," Darci said.

5

"We have really good horses here too," Lisa put in, shaking back her hair. "We go horseback riding at a neat stable right near here."

Darci had been wanting to go riding for ages. But she decided now was not the time to mention that she'd never been on a horse.

"Is the stable in Oakwood?" Darci said, hoping they would stay and talk some more.

"Yes, it is," the girl who wore glasses said.

"We better get going, you guys," Lisa said then. "The bell's going to ring soon." They started off down the hall, but as they passed a bulletin board, they stopped to look at a poster there. Darci caught up with them and paused too. The poster had big, colorful letters, and it said:

6th Grade
Dance
Contest

A little notice near the poster gave the time and place: April 27, PE class.

"Look at that," Lisa exclaimed. "They're finally going to let us have a dance too, just like the seventh- and eighth-graders. Doesn't that sound great?"

"It does," one of the girls agreed. "Why don't you go to it, Lisa?"

"Yeah, you should, Lisa," another friend said. "You'd win. Who's going to be your partner?"

Lisa shrugged and rolled her eyes. "Oh, I don't know."

They all moved off down the hall together in a huddle, and Darci heard them mentioning various boys' names and giggling as they went.

She stayed there gazing up at the poster for a minute.

A dance contest. That sounded like so much fun. She'd gone to dancing class last year at the Y for a while. Dancing was so great. She let her mind drift for a moment and imagined herself moving to the rhythm of some good music. But wait a minute. She'd have to have a partner. She'd need to know a boy who liked her and liked dancing —a nice boy who didn't play tricks on her and laugh at her.

She walked on down the hall, trying to walk sort of sideways so people wouldn't see her wet jeans. How could she get to know a boy? It was so much easier when you had friends. Then you could all get together and call boys on the phone. Or one of your friends might ask a boy if he liked you and help you that way. No way could she hope to do all that in a few weeks. But it was hard to get the thought of the dance contest out of her mind.

The Worst

When Darci reached her classroom, she headed straight for her desk. She slid into the chair with a sigh. At last! If only she could stay there until she was dry. The bell rang, and the rest of the kids drifted into the room, kids she didn't know unless she could count Lisa and Nathan. She almost wished Dad hadn't gotten this great new job in New York State that had caused them to move right in the middle of the school year way across the country. She knew Dad was sorry about the move, but he loved his new job.

Mom said new experiences were good, but they didn't feel good, not yet anyway. She also said the way to make friends was to get into things. But Darci knew that too wasn't going to be easy. If it weren't the middle of the school year, things would be different.

She saw Lisa and one of her friends sitting down at their desks now across the room. And there was Nathan coming her way. He sat right in the same row of seats she was in. What bad luck! Darci bent over her notebook, pretending to study her spelling list. Next to her, a girl squeezed behind her desk and began to stow away her books.

"P-s-s-s-t, Darci, are you dry yet?" she heard Nathan call to her.

She looked up at him. "No, I'm not," she said. How could one sixth-grade boy with curly black hair give her so much trouble?

"Look, I'm sorry," he said. This time he wasn't laughing, so maybe he really meant it.

She shrugged. "Okay, I believe you." She saw Lisa watching her from across the room. She probably wondered why Darci was even talking to Nathan.

Just then the teacher, Miss Sandor, came in, and they had to stop talking. The teacher was young, had short dark hair, and seemed okay. Darci liked her so far.

"All right, now, class," Miss Sandor began. "I have some news this morning." She smiled around the room. "We're going to put on our own television program." This school had a television studio with a TV set in each classroom, Darci knew. "We're going to do a science program about time and clocks tomorrow," she continued. "We'll have the talks some of you have already given to our class. I'd like to have Nathan give one and . . ." She mentioned several others. Darci wondered what it would be like to be on a TV program.

Just then Miss Sandor said, ". . . and I'll need someone to help me in the studio." She looked around the room, and a few kids sat up straight and looked eager. A couple half raised their hands.

Darci was just thinking that, of course, she wouldn't be chosen, because she knew nothing about a TV studio. Then to her amazement, she heard Miss Sandor saying, "I think I'll ask Darci to do it, since she didn't get a chance to be in on these science reports. Besides, we all know she has come here all the way from California."

Everyone in the whole class turned around and stared at Darci. She felt nervous. She hoped Miss Sandor wasn't going to ask her to stand up and give a talk right now about California or something.

"So for those reasons," Miss Sandor went on, "I'll ask her to be my helper."

Darci smiled her thanks at Miss Sandor.

Several of the kids made faces of disappointment, but Nathan turned to grin at her. When Miss Sandor wasn't looking, he zinged a rubber band at her that flew just past her nose. She tried to ignore him. He'd better not think she was pleased to be on the TV program because he was on it. That would be the last reason why she'd want to do it.

But it could be fun to go to the TV studio. This was one good thing that had happened in the new school.

At the midmorning recess, Darci hoped her jeans looked dry although she still felt damp. When she and the others all got up to crowd out of the room, no one said anything about them.

In the hall, she tried to catch up to Lisa and her friend —Blythe, she'd heard the teacher call her. But to her disappointment, she saw them go off with the same two girls they'd been with earlier that morning.

Several boys came up to her, smiling in a kind of funny way, and she thought, Oh, no, not some more tricks. But then a tall, blond one said, "Are you really from California? Did you ever go surfing?"

"No," she said regretfully, wishing she could tell them all about surfing, "but my brother used to go a lot."

"Oh, yeah? Lucky guy," he said. Just then, Nathan and some other boys called to him, and they all rushed off, yelling to each other about getting a kickball. If they'd waited, she could have told them about her older brother's new pet, a three-foot-long snake. She wasn't sure how much she liked this new pet of her brother's. It was a rainbow boa constrictor named Bo, but at least Bo was in a big glass cage.

At lunchtime, Darci kept looking for something to do and someone to do it with. A redheaded girl from class walked by.

"Hi," Darci said. "Want to play kickball or something?"

The girl stopped and smiled at her. "Hi," she said. She glanced around. "Well, maybe I could." But then she saw someone and waved. "Oh, sorry," she said. "I promised Wendy I'd meet her. She's my best friend, you know." And she ran off.

So that's the way it was. Everyone already had friends. The kids here didn't mean to be unfriendly, they were just already busy. Darci wandered through the playground. Once she ran to pick up a kickball.

"Need any more players?" she asked.

"No," the girl said. "We have too many now."

When the bell rang, Darci tried to blend in with the crowd as they all streamed back to the building.

Then the worst happened. That afternoon during physical education, the PE teacher, Miss Sturtz—who was tall with frizzy hair—chose two girls, Angela and Josie, to be team captains for kickball. Sometimes teachers would just count off for teams, but that didn't happen today.

These two girls began to choose, apparently their best friends first, then Lisa and her friend Blythe, then others. They kept picking and picking, the redheaded girl, her friend, Wendy, more and more. They passed right over Darci every time as if she were a rotten apple in a whole bowl of good ones. Finally only Darci and another girl were left. Angela chose the other girl, and Darci stood there all alone. It seemed like forever that she stood there. Sharp shouts from the boys' Frisbee game floated on the air. The traffic grumbled and mumbled by, out on Oak Avenue. It was a terrible moment all by herself like that.

Then Josie said, "I'll take her" and pointed at Darci. She didn't even say Darci's name.

Darci and Bo

Darci walked slowly down her street that afternoon. Forest Street. It had a lot of bare, leafless trees and white houses. Was this really her street where she lived now, in this new town without a single friend?

On down the street, she saw her six-year-old brother, Donny, skateboarding on the sidewalk. She turned up the front walk of her house. She wished there would be another letter from her friends today, but she'd just had a joint one from her three closest friends yesterday.

She opened the front door and stepped into the hall. There was her brother Rick down on the living-room floor, his long, sixteen-year-old body stretched out on the rug. He was shining a flashlight under the couch. What in the world was he doing?

"Rick, what happened?" She hurried into the living room.

Rick looked around at her, his face flushed. He was obviously upset. "It's rotten, really rotten."

"What is it?" But already she was guessing it must have something to do with that new pet snake of his.

Rick moved away from the couch to look under a chest. "Bo got out of his cage while I was at school. Now he's gone." Darci knew Rick had spent a lot of money buying Bo.

"You're kidding!" Darci looked around nervously. That three-foot-long snake was slithering around in here somewhere? "Where do you think he is? He shouldn't be that hard to see."

"You wouldn't think so, would you?" Rick sighed. "Here, Bo," he called. He had named the snake Bo because it was a rainbow boa constrictor, all smooth and rosy-colored, Rick claimed. To Darci, he'd looked more like brown.

Darci set her books on the couch and knelt to look under it. "Where's Mom?" she asked. All she saw under the couch were a few balls of rug fuzz.

"She's upstairs. She says she's already checked the whole house, and it's up to me to find him." Rick sat up and scowled. "I've searched everywhere."

Darci looked around the living room, so different from their living room back in California. It had the same furniture—the same big green chair, beige couch, green rug— but it didn't seem like home.

"I can't believe there's really a snake in here," she said. She didn't want to believe it either. The whole idea gave

14

her the creeps. Maybe if she'd had more of a chance to get used to Bo . . . but Rick had only gotten him last week, just since they'd moved here.

"I could help you look around some more," she offered. The afternoon lay like a big, empty nothing before her.

"Thanks, Darci." Rick went over to search behind a couple of large cardboard cartons that hadn't been unpacked yet. "Look every place you can think of, warm places especially, like near the radiators. He can climb up on things too, don't forget."

How could she forget that! She began to look behind the sofa cushions, then in the wastebasket, then up on the chairs. She peeked behind the radiator under the window.

"Where is he anyway?" Rick groaned. "And the guys are coming over in a minute too."

Lucky Rick had friends already. She couldn't help feeling envious. "Maybe they'll help you look for him." She could hang around with them, join in the search. That would fill up part of the afternoon.

Rick shook his head. "I've already looked everywhere. Besides, they want to play baseball." He went over to the fireplace and began to poke behind the logs in there.

Darci watched her brother. He was a tall, thin guy in a T-shirt and jeans, and he had a couple of pimples on his face and a few little rough places on his chin that he claimed needed to be shaved about once a week. Why did he have friends already? "Rick, how'd you get friends so fast?"

"Huh?" Rick took his head out of the fireplace. He sat back on his heels and looked at her seriously. "Well." He thought a minute. "Of course, some of the guys have cars, so it's easier to get around. Then there's this guy, Christopher, right here on our street who is my age. You've seen him. If we want to get up a game, we can ask the younger kids, Nathan and his friend Bill. Aren't there any girls around here?"

Darci shook her head. Actually, there were those two on the bus who might live nearby, the ones who didn't make room for her on their seat this morning. They seemed totally happy with each other.

"Well, try some sports. I'm getting to know the guys on a Frisbee team."

She couldn't bear to tell him how she'd been chosen last today. "I wish I could play ball with you this afternoon." She liked baseball too and had played softball in PE at her other school.

"Aw, Darce, it's going to be just the guys, ya know? And how would I look with my little sister hanging around?"

The doorbell rang suddenly. Rick stood up and headed for the door. "Hi, you guys," he called out as he opened the door. There was a burst of voices and laughter.

"Rick, let's go. Check out my new baseball, would you?" That was Christopher, the boy in Rick's grade who lived down the street.

"Okay, I'm ready." Rick sounded almost happy again. The door slammed shut behind him. The voices faded away. It was very quiet inside the house now. Darci stood up and peered out the window. Nathan and that other boy, Bill, were with them in the street playing baseball. Donny was crouched on his skateboard watching them. Donny had been sad about the move too, but Dad had let him buy some new goldfish. Donny was all excited about that. Darci sighed. Fish could never make up for friends. If she were back home now, she could just go to the phone and call up Luanne or one of the others and get one of

16

them to come over to visit her. But now—she checked the mail on the hall table, but of course there was nothing for her.

Darci started up the stairs slowly. Could snakes go upstairs, she wondered? She'd look around for it. But what if she did see it? What would she do? Grab a three-foot-long snake?

The stairs had brown carpeting, and the walls were dark, all so different from their last house. It was like living in a foreign country. Darci followed the dark walls up the stairs and down the hall to her parents' bedroom.

Mom was sitting on the bed, unpacking a box of clothes.

"Hi, Darci." Mom looked up with a quick smile. "How was your day at school?"

"It wasn't the greatest, Mom." Darci went over to sit on the bed.

"Well, it's bound to take a little time," Mom said sympathetically. "It's hard to be new, I know. Do you like your teacher?"

Darci began to help her mom unpack the clothes. "Oh, yes. Miss Sandor is okay. In fact, one good thing happened. She asked me to be the helper in the TV studio for a program on science talks."

"Good, Darci. That's the way to go. Get right in there and start doing things." Mom looked pleased.

Darci didn't have the heart to tell her about the terrible time she'd had on the bus with the water balloon, and how she'd been chosen last in PE. Mom was trying so hard to cheer her up.

"Did you get to know any of the other kids today?" Mom asked. "The best thing is to get into some school activities."

Darci remembered the dance poster. "Well, there's a sixth-grade dance contest in a few weeks. But I don't know any boys."

"Well, you will, you will." Mom smiled brightly. "That's a good place for a dance, at school. And you could always get Rick to practice with you."

"I know," Darci agreed. Getting some practice wasn't the problem.

"Maybe you could invite some girls over here," Mom went on, "or you could go to a movie on Saturday afternoon."

Suddenly Darci had an idea. She remembered her talk with Lisa and her friends about horseback riding. "Oh, Mom, I did hear of one thing. It wouldn't be at school, though. These girls were talking to me, and they said they do a lot of horseback riding. They thought I had too, because I come from California. Do you think—?" Darci began to feel excited. "I've always wanted to go horseback riding. Do you suppose I could? Would it cost a lot?"

"Good idea." Mom looked approving. "You could do it a few times anyway. Perhaps you could arrange to ride with those girls."

"Yes, that's what I was thinking." Darci jumped up. "I'll ask them about it tomorrow, where the stable is and all that."

Just then, the phone rang, and Mom began to talk to someone about an adult education class. Darci hurried out to the hall and into her room. She'd get out her horse books—read up on what it might be like to ride a horse —and tomorrow she'd ask Lisa and her friends about the stable. Maybe she'd even say, "Wouldn't it be fun to go together?" Better yet, maybe they'd say it first.

In her room, she turned on her clock radio and tuned

in to some good fast music. She danced a few steps and snapped her fingers. She'd loved dancing class last year. Could horseback riding possibly be as much fun? Now she had several good things to hope for anyway.

She headed for the cardboard box in the corner of her room and began to unpack her books. Here was her old diary. She flipped through the pages and the names of her old friends—and the cute boys she used to know—jumped out at her. If only there were some boys like that here. But she mustn't think about those past times. She didn't even want to write in her diary, because it reminded her too much of home. Right now, she'd work on her new plan instead. To ride on a horse, wouldn't that be terrific!

Darci unpacked all the familiar books and set them in a row in her bookcase. When she came to the horse ones, she stopped and sat down on her bed with them. Riding shouldn't be hard. All you did was put your foot in the stirrup, climb up into the saddle, and hold the reins.

What fun it would be—with four new friends maybe. She looked at the jackets of the books. What beautiful horses. Look at those dark eyes—velvety eyes, the stories always called them. Or was it noses? She could hardly wait to pat one. Never mind that she'd never really ridden before. She'd read so much about it, she felt sure she'd know how. She could just imagine herself on the back of that beautiful white horse, flying along. Yes, she would definitely ask Lisa and Blythe about it tomorrow.

Thinking about all this made Darci feel so good that suddenly she was hungry. She'd go downstairs and get something to eat. She jumped up and went out in the hall where she heard Mom still talking on the phone. Getting into things here was definitely the way to go. She'd be on the TV program tomorrow, and then maybe soon she'd be flying along on a white horse. And who knows, maybe somehow she'd get into the dance contest too. Darci hurried downstairs to the kitchen. She took peanut butter and bread from the cupboard, then turned to the refrigerator to get some milk.

She was just opening the door when she saw something move on the floor. It was a long, brown something, and it stuck out between the refrigerator and the cupboard.

"The snake!" she exclaimed out loud.

What should she do? Should she try to grab it? What if Bo didn't like being grabbed? But there was no time, no time! Bo might get away. She leaped forward. Just then . . . *whisk!* The tail disappeared behind the refrigerator.

"Come back here," Darci cried. She fell to her knees, tried to poke her fingers between the refrigerator and the side of the cupboard, but she felt nothing. Bo must be right in there somewhere. She jumped to her feet and headed for the front of the house. She yanked open the front door. The two high school boys and the two sixth-graders were in the street, and Donny was on the sidewalk.

"Rick, Rick!" she yelled, darting down the steps. "I saw your snake."

"What?" Rick stopped still just as he was about to throw the baseball. "You saw Bo?"

"Yes, hurry! He went behind the refrigerator."

"You're kidding!" Rick came running. "You're sure, Darci?"

"Yes. I saw his tail sticking out."

"What's going on?" the other boys called, and they came running up to her too.

"I tried to grab him, but he got away," Darci said.

"Hey, are you afraid of snakes?" Nathan grinned at her.

"Of course not." Darci tossed her head indignantly. "I tried to catch him, didn't I?"

"Oh, man, I hope he's still there." Rick raced into the house, and the others followed him, Donny last.

"Good. I hope you catch him," Donny exclaimed. "I don't want him to get my goldfish."

As they all pounded into the front hall, Mom rushed down the stairs. "What happened? You've seen the snake?" she asked.

"Yes, yes, Mom." Darci and Mom hurried after the boys.

But out in the kitchen, there was no sign of Bo, not even the tip of his tail. "He was right there"—Darci pointed to the spot—"and then he went *whoosh,* back of the fridge."

"Now what?" Rick moaned. "How can I get hold of him?" He crouched down and tried to peer behind the refrigerator. But the refrigerator was set in an opening between built-in cupboards, and it just barely fit.

"Maybe you could poke back in there with something," Christopher suggested.

"Yeah," Donny chimed in. "Here, you want a big knife?" He rushed over to the kitchen drawer.

"No, cool it, Donny." Rick frowned at him. "That would hurt Bo."

"Want us to try to pull out the refrigerator?" Christopher, who was a short, heavy guy, started to seize one side of it.

"Yeah, yeah," Nathan and Bill agreed. "We could all pull it out together."

"No, no thanks." Rick shook his head. "That might really squash him."

"The snake could have gone somewhere else already," Mom put in.

But Rick got a flashlight and tried to see behind the refrigerator anyway. Meanwhile, the rest of them searched all around the kitchen, but they didn't find him anywhere.

"Rick, that's such a shame. I know what this means to you," Mom said finally, heading out of the kitchen. "I'll be upstairs if you see him."

"Okay, thanks everybody." Rick let out a big sigh. "I'll set a dish of water on the floor. Maybe that'll bring him out. Would you keep watching for him, Darci?"

"Just call us if you see him." Nathan's black eyes seemed to be taunting her. "We wouldn't expect you to catch him all by yourself."

"I could." She sniffed. Actually she wasn't too sure about that, but she wasn't about to tell him. That Nathan with his crazy, curly black hair wasn't half as nice as the boys she used to know.

Rick glanced at the clock. "We better go finish our game."

"Yeah, yeah. Let's go," the others said. So all the boys, including Donny, who tagged along after them, headed for the front door. They slammed it behind them as they went out.

Now the house was quiet. Darci and Bo were on their own again. Well, never mind, she thought. She'd watch for Bo for a while. Then she'd go upstairs, look at her horse books, play her music, maybe even practice a few dance steps . . . just in case.

On Television

In the morning, Darci was up early so that she could spend plenty of time picking out just the right outfit to wear for the TV program. She almost wished she were giving a science talk too, so she could actually be on TV. Looking out the window, she saw it was another gray, cold day. She wished the sun would shine here.

She decided to wear a red sweater over a white turtleneck shirt and her dark blue jeans. She gave her brown hair a quick brush. Did she look okay, like someone the other kids would want to be friends with? Just think, maybe in an hour or less she'd be talking to Lisa about the riding stable and maybe making her first friends.

As Darci headed for the bus stop, she saw Nathan and Bill and another boy already there. When they saw her coming, they went into a huddle and started snickering. That made her mad. If they tried to put any more water balloons under her . . .

But there was the bus rumbling down the street, and Darci ran to catch it. By the time she climbed onboard, Nathan and Bill were already at the back of the bus. Luckily there was an empty seat next to an older girl. Darci rushed toward it and plopped into it, gratefully. The older girl was reading a paperback called *Moon Love for Maudy*. Darci looked around for the two girls in her class. There they were. She'd passed them on her way to her seat. They were a few seats ahead, sitting close, laughing and talking together. They were wearing matching lime green sweaters. It gave Darci a little ache in her chest to see them. What fun it would be to dress the same way as your best friend.

When it was time to get off the bus, Darci pushed through the crowd to get right behind the girls. If they looked around, she'd say hi and then they might get to talking. But nothing like that happened. Finally she did say hi to them anyway. But just then, they got off the bus and raced toward the red-brick school building.

Darci hurried from the bus for her third day in the new school. It was a big, gloomy building all right, and it was cold this morning. She shivered inside her wool sweater and looked around for Lisa and her friends.

"Darci!" a voice yelled right behind her. She jumped. It was Nathan. He and Bill and some other boys went rushing past her. She ignored them. That Nathan!

Inside, as she was heading down the hall, she saw Lisa and Blythe up ahead. She felt a sudden tightness in her chest. Should she ask them? But what else was there to do? No point trying to make friends with that redheaded girl —Anne was her name—because she was already best friends with Wendy. Or the two on the bus. They were all wrapped up in each other. At least Lisa and her friends had talked to her a little bit. Maybe it would be easier for a group to add one more. It was hard for two to become three. She'd ask Lisa about the stable. She walked faster, passing the dance poster. No time to look at that now. She made herself catch up with Lisa.

"Hi," she said, coming alongside Lisa and Blythe.

"Hi," they said, glancing toward her.

"Did you sit near Nathan again?" Lisa asked quickly, her blue green eyes bright.

"No, thank heavens." Darci breathed a sigh of relief loudly. Why did Lisa want to know about Nathan anyway? Quick! Start! she told herself.

"Could you tell me the name of that horseback riding stable you were talking about yesterday? I—I was thinking I might be going soon."

"It's the Cartridge Stable," Lisa said.

"Cartridge? Oh, thanks. I—I might go this Saturday or the next. Do you—uh—think you all might be going then?" This was really hard to do. She hoped they didn't think she was pushy.

"You mean horseback riding?" Lisa looked surprised.

"Yes. I thought if we were all going at the same time that'd be so much fun." There, she'd said it.

Lisa raised her eyebrows and glanced toward Blythe. "I don't know. We rode horses last summer in camp. But I don't know if my mom could take us this Saturday. She's the one who usually drives us there."

"My mom will be working," Blythe said.

25

"I'm pretty sure my mom could drive us," Darci said, really fast. She decided she would still skip mentioning that she had never been on a horse. "I'll ask her if she could do it if you think you could go." She looked eagerly at them.

"Could you take any more?" They had reached the door of their classroom now, and Lisa paused.

"Sure, we could squeeze in several more girls."

Lisa and Blythe exchanged glances.

"Oh, girls?" Lisa laughed. "Well, how about Jennifer and Patti?"

Those must be the others she was friends with. "Great! So you think you could come?" They still hadn't actually said yes.

"Maybe." Lisa tucked her hair behind her ear. "We were going to have a club meeting on Saturday."

"We could let her know later," Blythe put in.

Darci felt disappointed. She wished they'd said, "Oh, terrific! We'll do it for sure." But, of course, they'd have to ask their parents, and then there was the problem of their club meeting.

Lisa glanced toward the classroom, where a lot of students were already sitting at their desks. "I was afraid you were going to ask Nathan." She giggled. Then she leaned toward Darci and lowered her voice. "Say, have you thought of a way you could get back at him yet?"

"Not yet." Darci frowned.

Lisa had a little smile on her face. "You know how you're going to be on that TV program with him today?" Darci nodded, wondering. "Why don't you think of some way to make him do something funny when he's on it?"

"You could"—Blythe tittered—"in front of the whole school. That'd be so great. It'd be way better than listening to those dumb speeches."

Darci had to laugh. The idea had possibilities, all right. "I don't know just what I could do," she confessed. She waited a minute while some kids crowded past them to go into the classroom. "It could be funny," she added. "I can see that."

"You could cut him off in the middle of his speech," Blythe suggested.

"Show him blowing his nose," Lisa broke in. "Something like that."

Blythe laughed. "Yeah, that'd be great."

"Well, I don't know." Darci didn't quite see how she could arrange for that to happen. She glanced around uneasily, hoping no one could hear.

Lisa shook back her blond hair. "It'd be terrific."

The bell rang for classes then. Darci followed Lisa and Blythe into the classroom, thinking about what she could do to Nathan. She was thinking so hard, in fact, that she almost stumbled over his foot out in the aisle. She caught herself just in time. "Watch it," he said with a grin.

"Why don't you?" she retorted. That guy. Why couldn't he keep his feet to himself?

"Say, did you find Bo yet?"

"No." She'd really like to forget about Bo. She sank into her seat.

"Maybe he comes upstairs at night and slurps around from room to room." Nathan moved his hand in a snake-like motion.

"That's crazy." She glanced across the room and saw Lisa watching her. Lisa probably wondered why Darci would even talk to Nathan. "We think Bo probably escaped outdoors somehow."

"You hope!" Nathan laughed loudly. She glanced toward Lisa again. Lisa was right. It would be great if she could get back at Nathan. But how?

At recess, Darci wandered around, first outside, then she went in to get a drink of water in the hall. Then, of course, she had to go to the girls' room. Rebecca, the girl who sat next to Darci in class, was going in there just as Darci was coming out. Darci wondered if Rebecca had been getting drinks of water too.

"Do you want to play a game?" she asked Rebecca.

"Can't," Rebecca said. "I'm waiting for Margaret."

So everyone had a friend. Darci went out on the playground and watched some kids playing kickball. When someone ran near her, she said, "Do you need another player?"

The girl said, "Sure. Okay." So at least she got into a game for the rest of the period.

Then, as the bell rang and they were all going into school, Lisa came up behind her. "Got any good ideas yet?" she whispered to Darci. "You know, about Nathan?"

"No, I wish I did," she admitted. She could see that Lisa wanted her to.

Lisa frowned. "Too bad," she said. "Those programs are such a drag."

When the last period of the day came, it was time to go to the audiovisual room. As Darci and the others filed out of the classroom, Lisa rolled her eyes at Darci, and Darci knew what Lisa meant. She wished she could come up with something, so Lisa and Blythe would be impressed. Especially after Nathan edged up to her out in the hall and said loudly, "Still worrying about that big snake on the loose around your house?"

Josie and Angela were walking right in front of them. Josie looked over her shoulder. "You're kidding," she said, wrinkling up her face. "You've got a big snake in your house? Y-y-yuk! How can you stand it?" She said it as if Darci's whole family were all a bunch of freaks or something.

Darci felt embarrassed. Why did Nathan have to talk about Bo anyway? Why didn't Nathan just bug off?

Up ahead, Miss Sandor was turning into the audiovisual room. It was small and brightly lit. There were two TV screens and a large camera.

Miss Sandor had Nathan, Josie, and Angela sit behind a low table with a microphone on it.

"Now, Darci, come over to the camera." Miss Sandor showed Darci how to focus the lens and where the ON and OFF switches were. Miss Sandor went to a wall panel and pushed a button. The two TV screens flashed alive with light. Now the three at the table could be seen on the screens.

"Look, we're on TV." Angela laughed.

"Well, not in the classrooms yet. We're not transmitting now," Miss Sandor said. Angela waved to herself on the TV screen, patting her thick dark hair. "I look so funny."

"Well, you can't help it," Nathan said. "See, I'm a monster." He made a horrible face and flapped his arms.

Darci smiled. If only she could get him to do something like that on the program, how Lisa and the others would laugh.

"Enough, Nathan," Miss Sandor said. "Later, Darci, when we're ready to start, you push this lever. Then at the end of the program, when I signal to you, push the lever to OFF again."

Darci nodded. She was ready. Miss Sandor checked her watch. Nathan, Josie, and Angela sat still with their notes in front of them.

"I'm going to plug in the transmitter now," Miss Sandor said. "Then turn on the camera, Darci." Miss Sandor pushed a wall switch and pointed to Darci. Darci moved the lever on the camera, and a red light blinked on like a little red eye.

"Good afternoon. This is Channel KOS from Oakwood Middle School," Josie began. "Today we will have a talk on time clocks." Josie's face looked calm as she spoke, but Darci could see her foot under the table wiggling back and forth. When Josie finished, Miss Sandor pointed silently to Angela to begin. Angela sat straight and talked about sundials and ways of telling time in the past. They were all doing their best. No way could Darci trick Nathan into blowing his nose or anything else.

Then Nathan talked about natural rhythms and an experiment with some people who lived underground. As Darci stared at his image on the monitoring screen, she couldn't think of any way at all to trick him into anything. It was a crazy idea.

Now he was leaning toward the mike and saying, "Thank you for listening," and as he finished, he looked straight at Darci.

Miss Sandor signaled to Darci. Darci lifted her hand to the lever but as she did so, she made just the tiniest face at Nathan—Nathan who had caused her so much trouble. Nathan stared back at her, then, unbelievably, he stuck out his tongue. A big, red tongue . . . which was duplicated instantly on the monitoring screens and of course on all the sets in all the rooms in the school.

"Oh!" There was a gasp from the girls, and Darci was dumbstruck. She shoved the lever to OFF. The red light blinked out. But oh, wow, what had she done?"

"Well, Nathan," Miss Sandor said crossly. "I don't think that was quite necessary, do you?"

Nathan's face burned red. "I'm sorry, Miss Sandor. I—I thought it was turned off."

"Maybe—maybe I didn't turn it off fast enough," Darci exclaimed, overcome with guilt.

"That was no reason for Nathan to start making faces, was it, Nathan?"

"No, no, Miss Sandor." Nathan looked miserable.

"That was certainly no way to end a good program. The rest of you can go now. I think Nathan and I need to go down to the principal's office."

The principal's office! Darci followed the others out into the hall. She felt stunned. Why did her hand do that? How did she happen to make that face anyway? She should have told Miss Sandor that she made a face at Nathan, just a little one but enough to make him stick out his tongue.

The bell rang then, and all the kids came pouring out of their classrooms. Suddenly there were Lisa and Blythe and the others surrounding her.

"Darci." Lisa laughed loudly. "You did it. You did it. Oh, that was so fantastic."

"You know it." Blythe grinned. "That was the best TV program all year."

The whole group bunched around her, everyone looked so admiring. There was Jennifer, her glasses shining, and Patti, smiling at her. "All the kids in my class laughed like crazy," Patti said.

"It was pretty funny, wasn't it?" Darci had to smile too, just thinking about it. And yet, deep down inside, she had a little feeling of worry about Nathan.

Whose Idea Was It?

Darci hurried along the hall, carrying her books. So at least she had made a hit with Lisa and the others. She tried to feel good about it too. It had been funny, really funny, the way Nathan made that face on the TV program and the whole school had seen him.

Yet, she felt guilty. What was going to happen to him? Was he still in the principal's office? As she passed the office, she peered in. He was sitting on the bench across from the counter, hunched over a book on his knees, and he looked really down.

So, he was in trouble! But it wasn't her fault, was it? It was sort of an accident more than anything. Besides, look what he'd done to her. She tried not to keep worrying about it as she rode home on the bus.

After she got off, she walked slowly toward her house. It was cold here, and she shivered as she walked past so many white houses toward her own. Would it ever seem like home? It was all so different. Back in California, many of the trees stayed green all year, and the houses were mostly stucco, Spanish-style, and painted colors like pink and yellow and beige.

Just then, she saw Rick come out the front door of their house. Maybe she'd ask Rick what he thought about having to stay after school.

"Hi, Rick," she called. "Are you going somewhere?"

"Yes, down to Christopher's. Would you keep an eye out for Bo just in case?" They stopped on the sidewalk in front of the house.

"Sure, Rick." She looked up at her tall teenage brother and tried not to envy him because he had a friend nearby. "Rick," she said, "do you think it's very bad to have to stay after school? Have you ever had to do it?"

Rick shrugged. "A long time ago. It's not that bad, unless you're on a team and have to miss a game."

Did Nathan play on any teams? Darci didn't dare ask Rick if he knew.

Rick started down the sidewalk, then added over his shoulder, "I checked out three books on snakes from the library. I thought they might give me some hot tips."

"Good idea," Darci agreed. Anything was better than having the snake *slurping* around their house, as Nathan called it. She started toward the front door.

In the house, she paused in the front hall to look for mail. But she couldn't really expect another letter from her friends yet. She tried not to feel sad. She picked up Rick's snake books and thumbed through them. They seemed pretty good. She would read them later.

She heard Mom's footsteps overhead. "Darci." Mom hurried down the stairs. She was smiling. "I have a message for you. A girl named Lisa called. She wants you to call her back. Here's her phone number." Mom handed her a slip of paper. Mom looked pleased, and Darci knew it was because she thought now Darci had a friend. But Darci wasn't sure yet.

"Oh, good, Mom. I'll go call right away. I asked those girls about the stable, and they might like to go if you could drive us. Do you think you could?"

"Sure, of course, dear."

"Great, Mom." Darci hurried into the den and started to dial the phone. Maybe Lisa and the others would come horseback riding. As she dialed, she realized it was her first phone call from the new house. That was something anyway. A girl's voice answered.

"Lisa? This is Darci."

"Oh, Darci, that was so funny today about Nathan." How friendly Lisa sounded.

"It really was!" Darci agreed. "Nathan's in trouble, though."

"Oh, well, he'll get out of it. Listen, we're just holding a meeting of our club." A sudden hope swelled up inside Darci for a moment. Maybe they'd called to ask her to come over to join their club.

"We decided we could go horseback riding with you on Saturday if your mom can drive. We're pretty sure our parents will let us."

"Oh, Lisa, terrific!" Darci smiled into the phone. So

35

they couldn't ask her to join their club yet. They hardly knew her.

"Can Blythe and Jennifer go?"

"Yes," Lisa said. "Patti too. So what time and all that?"

"I'll let you know." Darci gripped the phone. They were coming! "I'll check it out with my mom and tell you tomorrow."

"See you tomorrow." The words sang in her head.

"Mom." She hurried toward the kitchen. "They can come, four of them, Mom. Is that okay?" Darci danced a few steps around the kitchen, snapping her fingers.

Mom beamed at her. "Good." But then she frowned a little. "I hope the horses are gentle and slow."

Darci paused to look at her mother. "Oh, I hope they aren't too slow." She felt sure those girls didn't ride old horses that just dragged along.

"Remember, you're only a beginner," Mom said.

"Sure. Thanks for driving us." Darci didn't feel like a beginner. She'd read so much about horses. She'd know just what to do. She'd get on that horse and fly along. Still snapping her fingers and humming, she left the kitchen. She'd have to write to Luanne about all this even though she had just written to her and the others last night and told them all about the dance contest and being the TV helper. Now she could tell them about what Nathan did on the TV program and how she was going horseback riding. They might not think she was so unlucky to have to move after all.

Darci ran up the stairs to her room. Things were looking so good. Quickly she wrote Lisa's number in her new phone book, stopping just long enough to take a fast peek under her bed for the snake. Then she settled down at her

36

desk and took out her stationery. Maybe after Saturday, she and Lisa and Blythe and Jennifer and Patti would really be friends. Friends! Everything was great now except—no, she wouldn't think about Nathan, sitting in the principal's office. Would he be mad about it? But what was one little stay after school? And look what he'd done to her. Still, maybe she should talk to him, tell him how sorry she was.

At lunchtime the next day, Darci saw Nathan walking by himself across the playground. Right after lunch, she had gone hurrying out there, hoping to get into another kick-ball game.

"Nathan," she called. "Wait."

Nathan turned to look at her, surprise on his face.

She hurried up to him. "I—uh—wanted to tell you." She stopped. This was going to be hard. How could she explain it when she hardly knew herself how it happened? "I'm really sorry about what happened yesterday on the TV program and all that. I guess I made kind of a face first. But Miss Sandor just saw you, I guess, and . . ." She realized something for the first time. He had not told on her. "You were nice not to rat on me about that."

Nathan shrugged. "Ah-h-h, that's okay." Was he looking a little embarrassed? She couldn't tell.

"Did—did you have to miss any games or anything?"

"Just the first part of a baseball game. It was only a practice game, though." He didn't sound mad at her. Maybe he figured it was just an accident, which it was in a way.

Suddenly a voice spoke behind them. "Hi, hi there." Darci turned to see Lisa, followed by Blythe. "Hi, Darci.

Hi, Nathan." Lisa's eyes sparkled at Nathan. "That's tough about yesterday when Darci got you in trouble, I mean."

Darci snapped her head around to stare in amazement at Lisa.

"Oh, well." Nathan started to grin. "So everybody got a good look at my tongue. I ought to charge them. I hope it wasn't coated."

"It was kind of funny." Lisa giggled. She turned to Darci. "You said you were going to get back at him, didn't you?"

"Oh-h-h." Nathan turned to look at Darci too, a new expression dawning in his black eyes. "You did, huh?"

Darci felt taken aback. "Well, I—I didn't know all this was going to happen," she protested. What did Lisa have to say that for? It was true in a way, but only in a way. "I was mad about the water balloon, but that TV thing was just sort of an accident. Maybe I didn't turn off the camera fast enough, though."

Still, Nathan was staring at her in that strange way.

"Anyway, Nathan, we thought it was really funny," Lisa said. "We just wanted you to know that. We didn't think you should have to stay after school."

Darci stepped back and let a crowd of kids pass by. How come Lisa didn't admit that it had been her idea too, her idea first, in fact? It didn't seem quite fair. Darci felt like telling Nathan that, and Lisa too, but she had a suspicion Lisa wouldn't like it at all if she told.

A Horse Named Lightning

Everything was going to be such fun—Darci's first chance to ride a real horse and make real friends. She had decided that whatever Lisa said to Nathan wasn't that important. She wasn't going to let it bother her. Nothing must spoil today.

But just as Darci and her mother were getting ready to leave, Donny said, "I want to go too." He turned on his fussy face, and Darci's heart sank. She didn't want her little brother hanging out with them.

"Oh, Mom, please don't let him come." How could she explain what an important day it was? They were all out in the kitchen, Dad and Rick doing the breakfast dishes, Mom and Darci putting on their jackets.

To her relief, Mom said, "Donny, I'll take you another time. Right now, I think it would be a good idea if you stayed here and helped Rick look around for that snake. You could look behind all the radiators in the house. He'd want to keep warm."

Darci had a feeling her mom wasn't too pleased about the thought of a snake that might still be in their house.

"Good idea," Dad said. "Donny, let's go have a big search."

Darci shot him a grateful smile. She knew he was trying to help her—knew he was sorry he'd had to move them all right in the middle of the school year.

She and Mom started off then in Mom's big used station wagon. Mom and Dad had decided they needed a car that could handle bad weather instead of the little Honda that Mom used to drive in California.

Darci sat up front with Mom, so there'd be plenty of room in the back. She closed her eyes for a moment. She could just see herself sitting on the horse, his mane flowing, her hair flying. They'd move together in one smooth motion. And the other girls would think she was really good, and later they'd all be friends, and . . .

"What's the number?" Mom peered out the car window.

Darci jerked her eyes open. "Uh . . ." She consulted the piece of paper she'd written the addresses on. "Eight-forty-five," she said.

Lisa was standing out in front when they pulled up at her house. It was a red-brick house with a lot of bushes out front. Lisa came hurrying down the walk wearing jeans and a shirt and a green-checked vest. She looked very horsey. Darci suddenly wished she had on something horsey too, instead of just her jeans and jacket.

"Hi, Lisa." Darci reached back and swung open the rear car door. "Mom, this is Lisa."

"It's really nice of you to take us to the stable, Mrs. Daniels," Lisa said. Her blond hair swung around her shoulders as she slid onto the backseat. "My mom couldn't drive us today. She was busy."

"We're so glad you could come." Darci's mother smiled over her shoulder. Darci knew Mom thought she was all set with new friends now. Darci hoped she was too, but she felt that today was more like a tryout.

"I hope I get a good fast horse." Lisa leaned back against the car seat and hooked a strand of hair behind her ear.

Fortunately Mom didn't say anything about hoping the horses were nice and slow. Maybe because she was busy driving through some traffic right then.

"I hope I have a good one too," Darci said quickly. "I just finished a book about a girl and her favorite horse."

"But there's nothing like really doing it," Lisa said. "At camp last summer, I had a black horse. He was fast and . . ." Darci decided not to mention a pony ride she'd had in the park one time. Lisa talked about her rides at camp until they pulled up in front of Patti's house, where Patti and Blythe were both waiting. Darci wished Lisa hadn't already done so much riding.

By the time they'd picked up Jennifer, they were all packed into the station wagon and talking all at once about their past riding experiences. Darci began to wish they were beginners like herself. Also, as they drove along, she wondered what was wrong with her stomach.

It felt so queasy. But the others seemed very excited, and then they began to talk about other people's rides.

"I knew a girl who was thrown off her horse one time," Blythe said.

"Well, my mom's horse ran away with her once," Patti said. "Did he ever go fast!" Patti was taller than the rest of them and good at sports, so she'd probably be extra good at riding. Darci's stomach felt tighter.

"Did you all go to the same camp last summer?" she asked, just to change the subject.

Mom turned the car off the highway onto a narrow dirt road, and they bumped heavily along past gray stone walls and trees.

"Yes, it was called Trail's End," Jennifer said. She straightened her glasses on her nose. "We got to ride a lot."

"We had dances on the weekend with the boys' camp," Lisa said. The others laughed.

"Lisa's really good," Blythe told Darci, "at riding and dancing."

Darci wanted to ask if they were all going to enter the dance contest, especially Lisa, but Mom was stopping the car now. They were in front of a low wooden building with a fenced corral out front. They all leaned forward to peer out the window at several large brown horses inside the fence. Darci wondered if it was the car ride that made her stomach feel so strange.

"Isn't this great!" Lisa exclaimed.

"You know it." Patti grinned. "I'm glad I didn't have to go to my dad's today." She turned to Darci. "He and my mom live apart. Usually he takes me miniature golfing or to the video arcade on Saturdays."

"Oh, swell," said Darci, weakly. She was not sure just

what to say. How would that be, to leave the rest of your family and all your friends every Saturday?

But now the girls started to climb out of the car.

"Mom, don't come back too soon," Darci said.

"Oh, I can't go yet, Darci. I have to speak to the man in charge. Now remember, be careful all of you."

"Yes, yes. We will." She didn't want her mother to talk about being careful in front of the others or to say anything about Darci being just a beginner. "Let's go look at the horses," she urged, darting toward the corral. The others hurried after her, but when she reached the fence, she stopped.

"Ah-h-h, look at them!" Lisa climbed up on the fence. "Aren't they neat? Here, baby. Here, baby!" She held out her hand toward one of the horses, and, incredibly, he began to walk toward her.

"Oh, Lisa, he's coming!" Blythe exclaimed. "He's terrific!"

"I love horses." Lisa leaned farther over the fence and reached toward the horse. "Come on, boy."

As the horse moved up to the fence, Darci found herself stepping back a bit. He was so large.

Lisa patted the horse's head and let him nose her outstretched hand. "Too bad I don't have something for you. There, there," she crooned. The horse lifted his lip and snorted, and Darci got a quick look at his teeth. They were yellowish and very big. She started to say what big teeth he has, but that would sound just like Little Red Riding Hood.

"He can probably tell I like him." Lisa patted the horse. "Can't you, boy? They know how you feel, you know." She turned back to the girls. "Like if you're afraid, they can sense it right away. Your body puts out a scent, and they can smell it." She snapped her fingers. "Just like that!"

Darci wished Lisa hadn't told her this.

"Darci!" Darci's mother was calling to them now and beckoning them over to the door of the stable. They all hurried on, and a man in riding pants and boots led them inside. It was quite dark in there. The man—he said his name was Mr. Hamlin—let them walk down the row between the stalls and look at all the horses. The horses' haunches seemed to loom up so high in each stall. And some of the horses didn't seem very friendly, the way they switched their tails back and forth and arched their long necks and rolled their eyes around to look at the girls.

When Mr. Hamlin and his helper began to lead the horses out into the yard, one of the horses snorted loudly and reared up in his stall. The whites of his eyes showed, and his hooves clattered against the wooden side. Darci suddenly wondered if she was going to enjoy this ride. Now she knew what was wrong with her stomach. She was scared! Would the horse know? But the other girls were climbing up in the stirrups and mounting their horses and calling out to each other.

"Mine's named Dobbins. What's yours?" Blythe shook back her short dark hair excitedly.

"Goldy. See how beautiful he is?" That was Lisa. She sat astride her horse so calmly and stroked his neck. Darci wasn't sure she wanted to stroke a horse. At least when Mr. Hamlin called her, she knew enough to go in front of her horse so he couldn't kick her.

"Oh-h-h, Darci, he looks terrific," Jennifer called out.

"He looks really fast," Lisa said.

Darci glanced up at him. He was very black, and with those long, skinny legs, why wouldn't he be fast? Why

44

hadn't she realized how big horses were? She walked over to his left side, the way the books said to, and put her foot in the stirrup.

"Your horse's name is Lightning," Mr. Hamlin said, hoisting her into the saddle.

"Lightning?" she quavered.

Mr. Hamlin smiled. "That's because he isn't. He's just the opposite."

Anyway, she wished she weren't riding a horse with that name. How far away the ground was. And with her feet stuck in the stirrups, she felt as if she were trapped way up high. It was like sitting on top of an elephant! Her body must be putting out that scent of fear Lisa had talked about, because her legs felt all watery. The horse could probably smell her fear.

Anyway, there were the reins. She picked them up and tried to act as if she knew what to do with them. She looked around at the other girls. "Great, isn't it?" she said, trying to sound casual. She didn't dare glance at her mother. Her mother would know that she was lying.

"All right," Mr. Hamlin said. "Now we're all going to ride out in a line. I'll lead, and we'll follow the path across the field and through those trees." He climbed up on his own gray horse and looked over his shoulder.

"Remember, tug on your reins to stop, pull the right one to go right, and so on. Ready? Give your horses a kick with your heels now."

Darci watched Lisa. Lisa gathered up her reins and quickly kicked her horse in the ribs. The other girls did the same, and they all began to move after Mr. Hamlin. Darci clutched her reins with sweaty hands. She dreaded kicking him. What if he didn't like it? But when he just stood there, she had to. She lifted her heels and kicked his sides.

For a moment, he turned his neck and looked at her with big dark eyes. Was he going to bite her foot with those big teeth? But then, amazingly, he too followed the others.

"Good-bye, Mom," she called with a quick glance toward her mother, who was over by the car now. Her mother was holding up her camera and snapping pictures. The girls were turning to one another with pleased smiles. This was really fun, wasn't it?

"Stop!"

The horses moved across the field slowly, with Mr. Hamlin's gray horse at the head of the line, the hooves going *clop clop* in the dirt. Riding was okay, Darci decided, clinging to the reins and trying not to slide around on the saddle as the horse jolted along under her. She was staying on anyway.

Mr. Hamlin was taking them on a path that led beneath bare trees. Some pale sunlight filtered through the trees, and a bird was chirping. As they rode in and out of the light and shade, Darci began to feel better and better. So what if she and the horse weren't galloping as if they were one? Maybe next time. Wait till she wrote to Luanne about this: *Went horseback riding today with four new friends.*

But now they were coming out on an open field again. Darci saw Lisa busily talking to Mr. Hamlin. Then Mr. Hamlin circled out from the line and called out, "All right, girls. Now we'll go a little faster."

Uh-oh! Did Lisa ask him if they could do that? A shiver of apprehension ran through Darci. Could she and the horse float along as if they were one?

"Give the horses a good nudge with your heel and call out 'Giddyap,'" Mr. Hamlin added. Lisa flashed a big smile around at the others.

The rest of them all called out "Giddyap," and the whole line started to trot at a faster pace. The girls' heads bounced along up front, their hair flopping up and down.

Darci clutched her reins nervously. What should she do? But, oh help, the horse was already doing it! He'd started trotting after the others. What a bumping! She grabbed at the saddle. The ground was whizzing by below her. Jolt, jolt! Smash, smash!

Now her right leg jerked loose from the stirrup. She stretched, trying to poke her foot in again, but she couldn't. She crashed up and down on the saddle and kept landing sideways. It was harder than ever to keep her balance. She tried to hang on with both hands. "Stop, Lightning, stop!" she shouted. Now the reins were sliding away. She lunged for them and that did it. She could feel herself slipping, slipping. . . . She went toppling over and around and down and *thump!* She landed backward on the ground. And as she looked up at the sky, she saw the horse's hooves practically sail right over her head.

Darci lay there for a minute. At least the horse hadn't stepped on her. How hard the ground felt. She sat up slowly. All the horses had stopped up ahead. Mr. Hamlin was coming back toward her. Her own horse stood a few feet away, eyeing her. How big he was from down here. She wished he'd stop staring at her.

"Are you hurt?" Mr. Hamlin said, riding toward her.

Darci stood up and dusted herself off and felt all hot and dumb while the others watched.

"Did you really fall off, Darci?" Lisa asked.

"Did you land right on your seat?" Blythe giggled.

"Are you okay, Darci?" Jennifer asked.

"I guess I am." She felt like a complete nerd! Falling off her horse like that. And her back and her elbow did hurt.

"Think you'll be okay?" Mr. Hamlin called down at her.

Darci nodded and straightened her jeans a bit and took a few steps. "Sure," she said. Actually she felt rather bruised, but she could still walk. She could walk all the way back to the stable, all right, and Mr. Hamlin could lead her horse. No way was she going to get back on that bumpy Lightning again.

Mr. Hamlin slid down off his horse. "Well, then, I know you're real eager to climb right back up there."

"I . . . I . . ." She couldn't quite blurt out her cowardly plan.

"These stirrups might've been a bit long," he continued. He bustled around the horse, tightening up the stirrups. Now she'd be really trapped up there. She wouldn't be able to fall out even if she tried. "Okay, come on, girlie."

She sure didn't want to get back on that horse. She saw Lightning roll his dark eyes at her. He probably didn't want her to get back on either. But the girls were all watching, and she saw Lisa and Blythe smile at each other.

"It's the best thing," Mr. Hamlin urged. "You gotta mount your horse again right away."

"He's right," Jennifer called out encouragingly.

How could she cop out here in front of everybody? She forced herself to walk over to Lightning and put her foot in the stirrup. She swung up on the saddle again, but she could feel the fear running all through her. Please, don't let me smell, she prayed. Don't let him know how scared I am.

They started riding again. This time they trotted more slowly, and Mr. Hamlin rode right beside her. That was embarrassing too. But she managed to stay in the saddle across the field and back down a dirt road, and she reached the stable with the rest of them.

"Guess you haven't done much riding," Jennifer said, reining in her horse beside Darci. "Sorry we went so fast."

Just then, Lisa rode alongside them too. "Goldy and I had such a terrific time, didn't we, old girl?" Lisa patted her horse.

"Sure beats miniature golfing," Patti called out from her horse. Yes, the others had all had fun. If only she hadn't made such a mess of things by falling off her horse.

They all got off their horses then, and Mr. Hamlin led the horses back into the stable.

"Don't worry, Darci," Lisa said to her. "You'll learn in time. It just takes some practice, that's all."

How much did it take? Darci wondered. In the meantime, she just hoped the girls wouldn't go off and laugh at her behind her back.

Maybe the horseback riding had done some good. Because on Monday, Lisa and the other girls sat with her at lunch—although Darci wished Lisa wouldn't keep mentioning how Darci had fallen off her horse.

Then, suddenly, while Darci was still eating her sandwich, Lisa stood up and said, "C'mon, kids, let's go."

Darci quickly crumpled her paper napkin and was about to get up too. But Lisa said, "Bye, Darci. We told these other girls last week we'd play volleyball with them today. We don't have any more room on the team."

"Let's move it," Blythe added, "or we won't get a ball."

"You're right," Patti agreed, and they started off through the cafeteria.

But Jennifer lingered. "See you later, Darci," she said.

"Jennifer!" Lisa called after her impatiently. "Come on!"

So they all left. Darci put the rest of her sandwich back in the wrapper. She didn't feel so hungry anymore. Still, at least they'd sat with her for lunch today. They couldn't help it if they had other plans. "Keep trying," Mom had said. Well, that's what she was doing. She glanced around at the other kids at her table. She didn't know any of them. They looked older, like seventh-graders. When the rest of the kids left the table, Darci stood up too so she wouldn't be left all alone there.

As she started out of the cafeteria, she saw redheaded Anne up ahead. She hurried to catch up. "Hi, Anne." She smiled.

Anne turned around. "Hi, Darci." Her face, covered with pale freckles, looked friendly.

"Are you going out to the playground?"

"Uh, sure. Where're Lisa and her friends? I hear you went horseback riding with them."

"Yes." Darci wondered if Anne had heard about her falling off.

"I see you with them a lot," Anne added.

"Yes, sometimes." Did Anne think they were her friends? Did it seem that way to the other kids?

"Do you like Lisa?"

"Well, sure." The way Anne asked that made Darci wonder. Did Anne like Lisa? Maybe Anne didn't understand how it was to be alone without a friend. Darci hadn't known it herself until she'd had to move.

Anne was glancing around at the kids on the playground.

"Can you play kickball for a while?" Darci asked quickly.

Anne shook her head. "I'm sorry. I have to meet Wendy. We always meet at lunch. She's my best friend." Anne frowned into the noonday sun, looking across the playground. "There she is, waiting for me. Good-bye, Darci. See you back in class."

Darci could understand. And now the other kids must think she was already friends with Lisa and her crowd. Mom said she could hardly expect to have best friends when she'd only been in Oakwood such a short time.

She wandered down the hall and stopped to look at the dance-contest poster again. It would be so much fun to be in the contest. Maybe she'd ask Rick to practice dancing with her tonight. Just thinking about whirling and swinging to the music made her forget for a moment about the problems of a new school and new friends . . . and first horseback rides.

"Hah!" Voices shouted suddenly behind her. She heard laughing and jerked around to see Nathan and a gang of boys. They were all grinning at her as they hustled past.

"Darci the dancer, eh?" Nathan teased, and they hurried on.

Darci's face flamed, embarrassed they'd caught her mooning over the dance-contest poster. That Nathan! Why did she have to know a boy like him?

A Good Sport

Darci had just finished lunch the next day and was throwing her paper bag in the trash when Lisa and Blythe came hurrying up to her.

"Darci." Lisa leaned toward her to whisper in her ear. "Do you want to do something fun?"

"Sure." Darci smiled. She'd been wondering if she could get into a game again after lunch.

"Well, come on with us then." Both of them had big smiles on their faces.

"What is it?" she said as they headed down the hall.

"Sh-h-h-h," Lisa commanded. "Just come. You'll see."

But they weren't going out to the playground. They

were going past the classrooms, slowing up for a moment to eye the poster about the dance contest.

"That'll be so neat." Lisa waved toward the poster.

"Sure, for you." Blythe laughed a little. "You know how."

"I do too," Darci added.

"Let's hope your dancing is better than your horseback riding, Darci," Lisa said, and she and Blythe laughed as they hurried on down the hall.

Darci guessed falling off a horse was funny, to some people anyway.

But now Lisa was turning into the girls' room. Darci suddenly felt worried. Is this where they were going to have fun?

Lisa rolled her eyes toward the stalls, where a couple of toilets were flushing. "Wait till they leave," she said in a low voice.

Lisa reached in her purse and pulled out a pack of cigarettes. So that's what Lisa had in mind.

"Lisa always has everything in her purse," Blythe said admiringly.

Darci raised her eyebrows, trying to look impressed. Actually, she didn't especially want to do this, didn't want to get into trouble in the new school. Besides, she'd already tried to smoke one time in Luanne's garage. The smell had reminded her of when their couch caught fire.

"Where are Patti and Jennifer?" Darci asked. "Want me to go look for them?"

"No, they're busy. Forget them." Lisa tossed her head crossly.

Darci wished she were busy too.

Lisa frowned into the mirror, and Blythe said, soothingly, "It's okay, Lisa. Who needs them?" Darci wanted to say she did and why didn't she go get them—anything to get out of here.

Lisa and Blythe began to wash their hands, running the water loudly until the other girls came out of the stalls. There were two of them. Darci glanced toward them, trying to think of some way out of what was coming. But no one spoke while the two girls brushed their hair and washed and turned to leave. One of them was Rebecca, who sat across from Darci in class. After they'd gone, Darci said, "Do you know Rebecca?" Maybe she could get Lisa to think about Rebecca instead of other things.

Blythe shook her head. "No. Who wants to? She's fat, isn't she?" Blythe wasn't all that thin herself.

"She's sort of a nerd." Lisa sounded scornful.

"I think she goes around with Margaret," Darci said.

Lisa waved her hand. "Forget about her. Come over here by the window. We'll just have time." She tapped out the cigarettes and gave one to Blythe. Then she offered Darci one.

Darci shook her head. "I'll just watch. I haven't smoked a whole lot." Once actually.

Lisa shrugged. "Okay."

"You should see Lisa blow smoke rings," Blythe said.

"Really?" Darci couldn't help being impressed.

"We both know how to inhale." Lisa put her cigarette to her lips, then she dug into her purse. "I'm sure I have matches." She frowned and brought out a handful of papers. "Oh, this is stuff my mom told me to take out of the car. Look, a Weight Watchers pamphlet. I ought to give that to Rebecca. Oh, rats! No matches?"

55

Good, Darci thought. Now we can leave.

"Ah-h-h." Lisa brought out two packs of matches.

"I knew you'd have them." Blythe held up her cigarette. Lisa lighted it, then her own. The two cigarettes glowed red. Swirls of smoke rose into the air and hung before the mirror.

"What if someone comes in?" Darci asked. She glanced toward the door. This seemed pretty dumb. It'd be a cinch to be caught.

"We throw our cigarettes in the toilet. That's easy." Lisa swung her blond hair back carelessly. "No problem."

The smoke was sneaking its way up Darci's nose and made her feel like sneezing.

"Don't you love it?" Lisa let out a great breathful of smoke, which blew right into Darci's eyes.

"It's the greatest," Blythe agreed.

But Darci's eyes were watering from the smoke.

"Let's see you blow a smoke ring," Blythe said to Lisa.

"Okay." Lisa took a deep draw on her cigarette, tilted her head back, and began to tap her cheek with her forefinger. With each tap, a circle of smoke floated from her mouth.

"See how she does it?" Blythe said to Darci.

"Uh-huh." Darci nodded. It would have been easier to see if her eyes weren't filled with smoke.

Blythe held up her cigarette eagerly. "I'm going to try it." She managed to blow out one circle of smoke before she had to let the rest drift from her mouth.

"Here, Darci, don't you want to try?" Lisa said. Darci had a brief glimpse of the three of them in the mirror—Blythe with her short, dark hair; Lisa's pale blond; and

56

Darci's own brown hair. Her face, her brown eyes, showed the way she felt—nervous.

"Me?" she said. But of course. Who else was in here?

"Come on. Here," Lisa said.

Darci frowned. "I was thinking about giving it up—smoking, I mean."

Lisa laughed. "Come on. It's safe here." She held up the cigarette to Darci.

"Well, okay." Darci decided she'd take one fast puff and that would be it. She'd get out of here. She put her lips to the cigarette and sucked in. But she couldn't help the tickle, the smell, the burning sensation in her chest like crawling ants. A terrible cough burst from her mouth, raking her throat, making her eyes water. She hunched over the basin, clutching her chest. She felt dizzy, grossed out. And now they knew she didn't even know how.

"Sh-h-h-h." Lisa laughed. "You need practice." She took back her cigarette.

"Uh-huh." Darci dreaded the thought. She scooped water into her mouth and aching throat.

"She's really a good sport, isn't she?" Lisa said, clapping Darci on the back. Before Darci could say that she didn't want to be a good sport any longer, there were loud grown-up voices outside the door. They stared at one another in horror. "Quick," Lisa hissed, "into the toilets. Lift your feet." As if smitten with a terrible need, the three of them rushed to the three stalls.

Darci sat down on the seat and raised her feet high. Oh, don't come in, she prayed. Don't. Please. I don't want to be caught. What if it was the principal? She waited, her heart thumping like crazy. Why did she ever get into this anyway?

But in a moment, the voices grew fainter. Darci wanted to leave—fast. "I think they've gone," she called out.

"Let's get going," Lisa agreed. The three of them came out of their stalls and met in front of the smoke-filled mirrors. Lisa went to the door and listened. After a moment, she said, "Okay, all clear."

They opened the door and hurried into the hall, where Darci took a deep, relieved breath of normal air. They were safe. There were no grown-ups around, only a few kids drifting past. But one of them was Nathan.

"What are you guys up to?" He came over to them. Darci froze. He couldn't possibly guess what they'd been doing, could he?

He said, "What are you looking so guilty about?" He sniffed. "Boy, do you stink!" He eyed them curiously, and suddenly his glance fell on Lisa's bulging purse. And there, sticking up, was the edge of the cigarette package!

Nathan pointed and laughed. "Oh, I get it. Working on your lung cancer, huh?"

"Be quiet!" Lisa pushed the cigarettes down into her purse. "You don't have to say that so loud." Then she smiled at him. "Bet you wish you had one."

"Oh, sure! Big deal! What a smell." He held his nose. "Pee-uuu!"

"You're just jealous," Blythe put in. Darci didn't say anything. Maybe he wouldn't take any notice of her.

"Here." Lisa extracted a little bottle from her purse and sprayed perfume on each of them. Then she pulled out some little tablets. "That'll make our breath okay too." She smiled brightly at Nathan. "Want one?"

"Yuk!" Nathan scoffed. "Say"—he turned to Darci with

a grin—"were you in on this too? Maybe I'll tell Rick." His dark eyes seemed to be taunting her. Darci chilled at the thought.

"Who's Rick?" Lisa asked.

"My brother," Darci answered. No use trying to be invisible any longer. "Look," she said, "please, Nathan, why don't you just forget about it?" This would sure be his chance to get even, though.

"Wel-l-l." Nathan grinned at her. "We'll see. Who knows?" He started off down the hall, then turned back to look at her again over his shoulder. "I'll think it over," he said.

Lisa turned to Darci. "I didn't know you had a brother. How old is he?"

"Sixteen."

"Oh-h-h." She raised her eyebrows. "And Nathan lives on your street, doesn't he?"

"I'm afraid so."

Lisa cast a quick look at Blythe. "Does he hang out at your house very much? He's a lot younger than your brother."

"The guys on the street play baseball together, that's all."

"Want us to come over some afternoon?" Lisa asked, her eyes gleaming.

Friends—to come over. Darci had been wanting that so much. But would they be doing that just because Lisa was interested in the guys? So what if they were? She'd show them how much fun it was over on her street.

"Why, sure," she said.

Then Lisa added, "We could get Jennifer and Patti to come too."

So it could be lots of fun anyway, Darci decided. "Okay," she said. "Let's ask them. How about tomorrow?"

"Help! Help!"

The girls were coming over tomorrow afternoon, except for Patti, who had a volleyball tournament. Darci was excited. Her first friends to come to the new house. So what if they were interested in the guys. It would still be fun. They could look at her horse books and her photo album and listen to music. She hoped they'd have a really good time.

That night at dinner, Darci said, "Some girls are coming over tomorrow."

Rick piled three pieces of chicken on his plate. "Want me to send up a cheer or what?" He grinned at her, though. "Are they the girls you went horseback riding with? Didn't I tell you sports was the way to go?"

She glanced gratefully at her mother. Evidently Mom hadn't told him about her falling off the horse. "Yes, Lisa and Blythe and Jennifer are coming." So far, Rick didn't seem to know about her smoking in the girls' room either, so she hoped Nathan was keeping quiet.

"That's good, Darci." Her dad looked approvingly at her through his wire-framed glasses. "You're making friends fast, I bet."

"I'm working on it, Dad." She knew he loved his new job and wanted all of them to like it here too. His company was trying to figure out why a bridge had collapsed, and every night he talked about it to Mom.

Rick said, "Too bad I can't find Bo. Your friends would probably like to see him." Darci wasn't sure about that. She didn't want to hurt his feelings, but she remembered how Josie had acted, as if having a snake was freaky.

"You can show your friends my goldfish," Donny offered.

"Thanks, Donny." But Darci knew she'd have to come up with something better for those girls than staring at goldfish.

Rick sighed. "That Bo was the greatest. He had a kind of rosy glow to him when I held him up to the sunlight. Oh, man—" Rick broke off and frowned. "I wonder if he's even still alive. If he's found water and a warm place somewhere, he'll be all right." Rick had searched the house again and again, even down in the basement, but with no luck.

"What if he gets hungry?" Donny asked, his mouth full of potatoes. "He better not go for my goldfish."

"Snakes don't eat that often, just every few weeks." Rick took a bite of chicken. "He might catch something on his own, mice maybe."

Darci remembered the little mouse in the cage up in Rick's room and suddenly decided she wasn't very hungry.

"I'm afraid Bo has probably snaked his way outside by now anyway, Donny," Dad said. "In which case, he probably died from the cold."

"Yeah," Rick groaned. "Poor Bo."

"It is too bad," Mom said, then she turned to Darci. "Darci, dear, about tomorrow. I'm so glad you're having friends over, but I'm supposed to go to my first Jazzercise class in the afternoon. And so I'll need one of you to keep an eye on Donny."

"Oh, no!" Darci stared at her mother. "You mean I have to take care of him?" That could wreck her whole afternoon.

"Maybe Rick will be home." Mom looked hopefully at Rick. "I really hate to miss the class. This nice woman I met at the PTA meeting is going to be there too." Mom was trying to make friends too, Darci realized.

"I don't need anybody to take care of me." Donny scowled.

"Yeah, you do," Rick said. "Okay, Mom, I'll look after the kid."

"Darci, I'm sorry I won't be here," Mom went on. "But I know you and the girls will have a good time.

But that was just the problem. Would they? Darci worried about it for the rest of the evening. Tomorrow had to be a good day. It just had to be.

The girls came at about four the next afternoon. When Darci opened the front door and found the three of them standing on her doorstep, she suddenly felt hopeful. Of course, everything was going to turn out all right.

"Come on in." She smiled. Out in the street, Rick and his friend Christopher, Nathan, Bill, and even Donny were all playing baseball. "Come on up to my room."

"Well, okay," Lisa said. "Maybe we could go outside later."

"Sure," Darci agreed. She closed the front door. They all stood in a bunch for a moment in the front hall, pulling off their jackets and putting them in a heap on a chair.

"Let's go upstairs," Darci suggested.

They clattered up the dark stairs, suddenly noisy with the sound of so many feet, her friends' feet. Couldn't she call them friends now? "Want to see my horse books?" she asked. "And the pictures my mom took of us at the stable?" She led the girls down the hall to her room.

"What a nice room," Jennifer said, looking around at the white curtains, the slanted ceiling, the flowery though faded wallpaper. It isn't a bad room, Darci thought. She felt kind of good about it. It was bigger than the one in the old house.

"Here're the pictures of our ride." Darci spread them out on her bed. Lisa bent over to look at them.

"Oh, terrific!" Lisa beamed at one of herself sitting astride her horse. "Hey, look at this one!" She laughed loudly. It was one of Darci, but neither her head nor the horse's head had quite made it into the picture.

Darci laughed too. "My mom sort of missed a few things," she agreed. But, in a way, she didn't like Lisa laughing at Mom's photography.

Darci snapped on her radio to some good fast music.

"Good music," Lisa said. She began to swing her arms and hips in time to the rhythm.

"Who's your partner going to be in the dance contest, Lisa?" Blythe asked.

Lisa pushed back her blond hair carelessly. "Haven't decided yet."

Darci was impressed. Evidently Lisa didn't have to worry about having a partner. Darci could see that Lisa would be a good dancer too.

Lisa gestured toward the window. "Maybe someone out there." She smiled knowingly toward Blythe. Darci was astounded. Did Lisa mean Bill or . . . or Nathan? She must be kidding!

Lisa suddenly stopped by the windows and lifted the white curtains. "Where did all the guys go?" She motioned toward the street.

"Maybe they went down to Christopher's," Darci said.

"H-m-m-m," Lisa said. "Why don't we go outside too? You know, get some fresh air and all that." She was smiling in a funny way. "Maybe wander down that way."

"Sure." Blythe jumped up off the bed.

"How come this sudden interest in the outdoors?" Jennifer laughed, her glasses glinting in the afternoon sun coming through the windows.

Lisa was interested in the boys, all right. "Sure, we can go outside," Darci agreed. If that's what they really wanted to do, well, sure, she was willing to go along with it.

"Great!" Lisa said. "Let's go." So Darci led them back downstairs although she still wished in a way they'd just stay up in her room.

"Want something to eat before we go out?" She paused in the front hall.

"Sure," Blythe said.

"Just something quick," Lisa added.

"Okay, we've got some apples and bananas, and . . ."

Darci started toward the kitchen. But then Lisa said, "Where's the bathroom, Darci?"

Darci showed Lisa the downstairs bathroom and led the other two to the kitchen. "Want some peanut butter?" she had just asked, when there was a loud scream.

Darci stood still. "What was that?"

"Help, help!" It was Lisa's voice. "Darci, come here!" Now her feet were pounding toward the kitchen. They rushed to meet her.

"Darci!" Lisa stood there, her blue green eyes wide. "I . . . I can't believe this, but there's a snake in your bathroom!"

"A snake?" the others echoed.

"Oh, no!" Darci stared at Lisa. "Rick's snake!" Bo had turned up at last.

"Yes, yes . . . I can't believe it." Lisa's voice was high. "I swear I saw a snake . . . in the toilet!"

"The toilet!" Darci exclaimed. She rushed toward the bathroom, the others right behind her. Yes, sure enough, there was a big snake all right, coiled up in the bottom of the toilet bowl.

"Oh, man!" Blythe said in a shaky voice behind her. "She wasn't kidding."

"I . . . I almost sat down there." Lisa's voice was scared and accusing.

"I think that's Bo," Darci explained.

"Who?" Lisa practically screamed. "You know him?" Her eyes bulged in amazement.

"Yes, well, you see, I think it's my brother's snake, a rainbow boa. Rick lost Bo a while ago around the house."

"Around the house? You're kidding." Lisa drew back.

"Oh, yuk," Blythe said.

"I can hardly believe it." Jennifer's eyes were big behind her glasses.

"Let's get out of here," Lisa added.

"Look, it's okay. He's not poisonous or anything. But, oh, how— What am I going to do? I can't let him get away."

"Maybe he'll just stay there until your brother gets back," Jennifer suggested.

"Oh, I don't know." Darci groaned. "The guys just left, so it'll be a while."

She peered into the toilet again. Bo had slipped farther back toward the pipes. "What can I do?" He could just slide away down that pipe, and Rick would never forgive her. And Nathan would say she'd been afraid and . . . "I've gotta do something," she burst out and fell on her knees beside the toilet. She dipped her hand into the water.

"You're going to touch him?" Lisa exclaimed.

"Well, yes. How else can I get him?" She didn't take her eyes off Bo as she slowly reached toward him.

"He won't hurt you?" Jennifer asked in a worried tone.

"I . . . I don't think so." Darci closed her hand around the coiled snake. "There, Bo, don't bite," she said in a shaky voice. "I'm just going to pull you out and put you in your cage now." But she couldn't get him loose. He was stuck too far down in the pipe, and she didn't want to hurt him. She plunged her other hand in, tried to scoop him up. "I just can't get him out of there. He won't budge." She felt frantic. She sat back on her heels, holding her dripping hands up in the air.

"Darci, that's so gross," Blythe exclaimed.

"I have an idea. Flush the toilet." Lisa laughed. "Get rid of him."

"I can't do that to Rick's snake," Darci protested. "That would be really bad for Bo. Rick would be furious, too."

But Darci was thinking about an item she had read in those snake books of Rick's. "Say, I just remembered something." She jumped to her feet. "I know what. You see, he'll have to stretch up out of there to get some air. And when he does"—she looked around at the girls' faces —"I'll grab him."

"Oh, wow!" Lisa shuddered. "I don't know if I'm going to stay or not." But she moved closer to the toilet.

"Let's just wait," Darci said. "Let's be quiet so he won't be scared."

"He couldn't be any more scared than we are." Jennifer rolled her eyes and giggled. "If you catch him, what are you going to put him in?"

"Oh, good idea, Jennifer. Would you get me his glass cage? It's in the den. I'll stay here and watch him."

The girls got the cage and brought it into the bathroom and set it on the floor. Lisa went and looked out front for the boys and reported there was no sign of them. Then they all hovered over the toilet and waited and waited. Still nothing happened. At least Lisa didn't say anything more about leaving.

"I'm sure I'm right about how he'll have to breathe air sometime." Darci frowned.

"Maybe it'll be hours," Blythe said.

"How long's he been loose?" Jennifer asked.

"About a week." Darci looked at the circle of faces. What could she do? She had to stay here with the snake. But maybe this was getting boring for them.

"He was cruising around your house for a week?" Lisa said. "I'd move out."

"Well, we kept looking for him. We were afraid he might have gotten outside."

All of a sudden, Bo lifted his head. "Look!" Darci whispered. Bo began to unwind and stretch a little. Oh, was it going to happen? Suddenly Bo darted straight up, up, higher, higher now for air. And *zip!* Darci lunged forward and snatched him near his head, just the way the book said. And she eased him up into the air as he slowly uncoiled himself, splashing and spilling drops of water everywhere. It had worked!

"Great, great!" All the girls were laughing and cheering. Darci opened the cage and carefully placed the long, glistening rainbow boa down into it.

"You did it, Darci," Jennifer and Blythe exclaimed.

"Yes, Darci, you were terrific." Even Lisa nodded in admiration.

Darci stood there, beaming and feeling relieved, when she heard the crash of the front door and the boys' voices. They were back!

"Look, look what we did," Lisa shrieked, running out toward them. "We found the snake in the toilet. We pulled him out."

Then the whole gang of boys rushed into the bathroom. The bathroom was full of people. Everyone was talking, asking questions. Darci and the other girls were all busy explaining. Rick was so happy. He had a huge smile on his face. And Nathan actually looked impressed.

"Did you really grab that snake, Darci?" he asked her twice.

"Yes," she said proudly, "I did."

She was just ready to lead the girls outside when Rick said Bo was probably hungry and that he was going to feed him. They all followed Rick into the den, where he set the cage on the table.

"What's he eat?" Lisa asked.

Darci knew what was coming, and she didn't want to see it.

"Is he getting the mouse?" Nathan asked her as Rick left the room. So Nathan knew too.

"The mouse?" the girls echoed.

"The snake eats mice," Darci explained.

"Ew-w-w-w," Lisa groaned. "That sounds gross." So maybe Lisa wouldn't think it was so much fun here after all.

"Well, he has to eat something." Darci defended Bo. "Do you want to go outside instead?"

But now Rick was back with the mouse in a small cage.

"You're actually going to do it?" Lisa asked. "I'm not watching." But she leaned forward eagerly to stare at the snake.

Donny screwed up his face as if he might cry. "I'm going upstairs to see my fish." He rushed out of the room.

"Let's leave," Darci said to the girls again, but no one moved. They all watched as Rick put the mouse in the snake's cage. But Darci didn't want to look, and as the snake slowly wrapped himself around the mouse, she shifted her gaze out the window. She'd had to do so much this afternoon. She didn't have to look at this too, did she? Besides, one quick, horrified glance showed her the mouse disappearing headfirst into the snake's mouth. She noticed Nathan was staring down at his shoes.

It would be over in a minute, and they'd go outside and

start having some fun. And casting a quick look around the circle at the girls' faces, she knew they were having a good time here today—knew the afternoon had turned out okay after all, and that was what mattered most.

Bo Goes to School

Rick was happy about Darci's catching Bo. The following week, he took Bo to school to visit his biology class.

"Bo made a real hit," he said that evening at dinner. "Everybody was wild about him. You should have seen the kids crowding around afterward. Man, was that Bo popular!" He dug into his baked potato.

"I wish I could take my goldfish to school," Donny said.

But Darci was still thinking about what Rick had said. "Rick." She put down her fork. "Did the kids talk to you a lot about him afterward?"

"Yeah, you know it! All the rest of the day. They even took a picture of me holding Bo for the school paper."

That was all Darci needed to hear. "Listen!" She leaned

toward her brother. "I just got the most terrific idea. Would you let me take Bo to school to show my class?"

"Wel-l-l . . ." Rick looked a little worried. "Maybe some guy would hurt him or let him loose or something."

"Oh, Rick, I'd watch him. Every minute. It'd be so great."

"Well, maybe." Rick took a big bite of potato.

"What an interesting idea," Mom exclaimed. "And I could take Bo to school in the car and pick him up right afterward, so he wouldn't be there long. What do you think Miss Sandor would say, Darci?"

"I could ask her tomorrow. Okay, Rick?" She looked hopefully at her brother. Wouldn't he understand why she wanted to take Bo?

"I wouldn't want anybody to mess around with him." Rick rubbed his chin as if he were worried. Or was he trying to find some whiskers on his chin? He thought he was pretty important these days because he had to shave once a week.

"I'll bet the teacher agrees." Dad smiled at Darci. "Keep at it, Darci." Dad understood what she was trying to do. "After all, where would Bo be if it weren't for Darci?" Dad turned to Rick.

"Oh, yeah, yeah, I get the point," Rick agreed. "Okay, you can take him. I'll let you use the wire carrying cage I just made."

"Oh, super. Thanks!" Darci said gratefully.

"Someday, can I take Bo to school?" Donny put in.

Darci was so excited about her plan she wrote another letter to Luanne that evening even though Luanne still hadn't answered her last one. She used to write in her diary a lot, before she'd moved, but these days it was more fun to write letters. She told Luanne all about finding Bo in the bathroom and the girls coming over. And how they might be her friends now and how she might be taking Bo to school. She didn't tell how lonesome it had been walking around school all by herself. But she did end the letter by writing *I miss you, Luanne. I wish you lived here too.* She closed her eyes and thought for a minute how great it would be if she had her old friends back. But what was the use of wishing?

The next day, Darci asked Miss Sandor if she could bring her brother's rainbow boa constrictor to school. Miss Sandor looked a little surprised, then she laughed. "A snake? How big?"

"He's only three feet long, and he'll be in a cage. He doesn't hurt anybody. He's a pet, you see."

Miss Sandor was silent for a minute, then she said, "All right, Darci. It'll be part of our science class tomorrow. Perhaps you could give a little talk about him, and when you're through, your mother could come and take him home again."

Darci was thrilled. She began to spread the word that day. "I'm going to bring my brother's pet snake to class tomorrow," she told Anne during recess, and Josie, and of course Lisa and the others. She leaned across the aisle and told Rebecca too. Everyone laughed and seemed to like the idea. Several of the kids talked to her at lunch about it. She could just see herself tomorrow, surrounded by Lisa and Blythe, Angela and Rebecca, Anne and Josie, and, well, yes, maybe some of the boys too. She might even get to know some boy, maybe even a boy who knew how to dance.

She worked on her talk that night and read two more snake books of Rick's. She'd tell about feeding Bo and how he'd escaped. It was going to be so exciting. And the other girls, especially Lisa and her crowd, would all want to sit with her and be friends, even if they did have their own friends already.

The next morning it was raining, their first rain in New York. April showers, Mom called it, but it looked like a real downpour. Rick began to make a big deal about Bo getting wet until Darci pointed out that he'd been in lots of water already.

Science class was last period in the morning. Mom was supposed to bring Bo just before class. "Hey, Darci," Nathan called back from his desk. "These guys don't believe you're going to show us a boa constrictor today!" Mike and Ted and Wally looked back at her questioningly.

"Are you kidding?" Mike asked, rolling his eyes. "A real boa constrictor?"

Darci shook her head, smiling. "No. You'll see. For science class. My mom is bringing him. He's a rainbow boa."

"What's he eat?" Wally wanted to know.

But Miss Sandor walked in then and raised her hand for silence. "Class, we're going to have a special treat today. Darci will have her brother's pet snake here, and she's going to tell us about him. But we have to get our work done first."

It was hard to keep her mind on the spelling and arithmetic that morning. Darci kept worrying about her talk, what she'd say. Her stomach felt tight. She remembered how Lisa said the science talks on TV were boring.

Finally it was time for science class. And there was Mom, knocking on the door and bringing Bo in his cage. A loud buzz went around the class.

Darci got up and walked over to her mother.

"Thanks, Mom," she whispered and took Bo's cage.

"Go to it, Darci," Mom whispered back.

After Mom left, Miss Sandor said, "Now class, let's quiet down."

Some of the kids in the back row were standing up so they could see. "And sit down too," Miss Sandor added. "Darci, are you ready?"

Darci nodded. She looked at the faces and tried to stay cool. This wasn't going to be that easy, to make a good speech. Everyone was watching—Lisa, Blythe, Josie, Rebecca, Mike, Ted, Nathan. That Nathan rolled his eyes at her and almost made her laugh.

She began. "This is Bo"—she pointed to the cage— "my brother's rainbow boa constrictor." Her mouth was so dry her tongue made loud sticky noises. "He's curled up now, but he's about three feet long."

"O-o-o-h." A slight gasp swept over the class. That made her feel better. So maybe they were interested. At least everyone was looking at Bo.

"The other day," she began. She talked about how Bo got loose and was cruising around the house somewhere. All eyes were on her. She was still a little scared, but somehow her mouth kept on talking—about how Bo was found in the downstairs bathroom; how he ate live mice ("ew-w-w-w," the class groaned); how sometimes snakes get ticks and how her brother put No-Pest strips in the cage; how snakes could live to be twenty years old ("twenty years," the class echoed); how Bo had tiny curving teeth, but not fangs because he wasn't poisonous; and how he looked kind of rosy in certain lights.

"Take him out of the cage," Wally begged, "and hold him up so we can see him better."

Darci hadn't planned on doing that. She'd held Bo only

a couple of times, not counting the day when she'd pulled him out of the toilet. And Rick had always been right there. She glanced toward Miss Sandor. "Well, I . . ." She paused.

"How do you feel about that, Darci?" Was there doubt in Miss Sandor's voice? "Do you mind?"

Darci saw Lisa looking at her with a little smile on her face. Well, she wasn't going to look afraid, not for anything. "Okay. I've held him at home."

Darci opened the cage door and reached in and gently eased Bo out in her hands. "It's all right, Bo. It's okay," she murmured, hoping not to startle him. She held him up with both hands. Bo extended his head out into the air and stared down at the class with dark slits of eyes.

"Look at him!" everyone exclaimed. Bo slithered around Darci's arm, winding around it like a bracelet.

"Look at that, would you? Look!" The kids were all half out of their seats.

"That's wonderful, Darci. Now put him away," Miss Sandor said. Darci pulled Bo off her hands and arm and set him back in his cage. That had been the hardest part, holding him. But at least he didn't bite her or try to get away. The class was clapping and smiling at her. And now Darci went back to her desk and sank down in her seat, warm, a little shaky, and relieved.

Miss Sandor talked to the class some more, first about snakes and then other living things, like insects and mice and so on. Finally the bell rang for lunch.

As they all crowded out of the classroom, Darci found herself surrounded by a tight group of kids. She picked up Bo's cage, and the crowd around her grew larger. Everyone had questions.

"How often do you have to feed him?" Mike asked.

"Where'd your brother get him?" Ted wanted to know.

"Say, Darci, can I touch him? Just with my finger?" That was tall, yellow-haired Wally.

"He's neat, isn't he, you guys?" Nathan put in. And it seemed as though all the boys in the class were bunched around her. All the boys! But where were the girls? A few pressed in on the outskirts. She caught a glimpse of Anne's red hair, and Rebecca trying to peer around the boys, and Angela. But the boys crowded in so close. Darci started to walk to the door.

Lisa tried to join them. "You should have seen him when he ate the mouse," she said loudly. But the boys ignored her and kept asking Darci questions. They stayed huddled around her in a tight circle, watching Bo in his cage and bombarding her with questions. She managed to get out of the classroom to go meet her mother. The boys stuck to her like flies, all the way down the hall and out to the parking lot. Mom was just getting out of her old station wagon and coming toward her.

Darci handed Mom the cage. "Thanks, Mom. Bo was a big hit."

"So I see." Mom smiled.

The boys all ran off then to lunch, and Darci hurried back down the hall toward the cafeteria. She was sorry the girls had been crowded out by the boys, but now she would find Lisa and the others. She hoped Lisa and Blythe had liked her talk and had saved her a place. And it would be fun to tell Patti and Jennifer about it too.

Darci entered the cafeteria. "Hey, Darci." Two boys she didn't even know called to her from a table. "We hear you had a snake at school. What's he like?" She stopped at their table for a minute to tell them about Bo. More boys wanted to ask questions too, but she moved away, looking

78

for Lisa and her friends. Ah, there they were, seated at one of the tables.

"Hi, hi." Darci rushed over to them. "At last! I finally got rid of Bo."

Lisa turned and looked up at her in a funny way. "Well" —she tossed her pale, blond hair—"at least you didn't get rid of the boys."

Darci stared at her. "The what?" she said.

"The boys." Lisa's blue green eyes were scornful. "I guess that's one way to make yourself popular."

Lisa turned her back on Darci and began to talk to Blythe and some others at the table in a loud, high voice about the dance contest—how there would be two eighth-graders as judges and prizes for the winners.

Darci felt sort of sick. Was Lisa jealous? And the others? There didn't seem to be any room for her at the table. She looked desperately around the cafeteria. Anne was sitting with her friend Wendy. And Josie was sitting with her friend Angela. And the tables were all full, and of course no one else had saved her a place.

"Hey, Darci," some of the boys from the next table called. "You can sit over here." But they were grinning as if it were a big joke.

But then Jennifer called out, "Here, Darci" and squeezed over at her end of the table. "Come, sit by me. I hear you gave a great speech."

So that was really nice of Jennifer, and Darci went and sat with her. But Lisa ignored Darci for the rest of the lunch period and never spoke to her again that day.

Weight Watchers

The next day at recess, Darci saw Lisa and her crowd standing together on the playground. Darci wasn't sure she wanted to go over and join them. But just then, Jennifer, with her round, friendly face and shiny glasses, beckoned to her. Well, anyway, Jennifer wanted to see her.

Then Lisa glanced toward Darci too. She didn't look cross anymore. "Darci, listen, we're playing a guessing game," she called. So Lisa wasn't going to mention Bo or any of that. "Want to play?"

"Well, sure." Darci went over to them. "What's it about?"

Lisa rolled her eyes toward a group of girls on the

playground. One of them was Rebecca. "How much do you think she weighs?"

"A lot." Blythe laughed.

"No, really," Lisa persisted. "Do you think she weighs about five hundred pounds maybe? I mean, I only weigh eighty-five pounds. What do you weigh, Darci?"

Darci glanced down at herself, her striped top, her jeans. She'd just as soon weigh a little more. "About eighty, I guess." Actually, it was less than that. She wished they were playing some other kind of game.

"Rebecca ought to go to Weight Watchers," Lisa added. "Like my mom. I still have that little folder about Weight Watchers in my purse. I ought to give it to Rebecca."

Someone had thrown Rebecca a ball, and she ran to catch it. As she charged across the playground after it, Lisa turned to the others and said, "Look how she jiggles." Lisa and Blythe burst out laughing, but Darci turned away, hoping Rebecca wouldn't realize they were laughing at her. Darci wondered if it was as hard to lose as it was to gain. She was always wishing she could add a few pounds, but that wasn't easy either.

Rebecca had the ball now and was holding it, looking for someone to throw it to.

"Rebecca, throw it here," Lisa shouted in a bossy way. Rebecca raised her arm, but then her glance passed right over Lisa and paused at someone else, and she threw the ball off in that direction.

"Well, so who wanted the ball anyway!" Lisa jerked her head back crossly. "She's a real nerd."

Darci guessed Rebecca had seen Lisa and Blythe laughing at her.

They started walking across the playground. Lisa

shrugged. "Forget her. What a blob! So how's Bo, Darci, and everybody else?" Lisa rolled her eyes. "All those cute guys?"

Darci had to laugh. "You don't mean Bill and Nathan, do you?" Nathan the pest? But then she remembered how Lisa had told him she was sorry he'd gotten into trouble on the TV program. And how she'd enjoyed herself over at Darci's house. Lisa must mean the older guys.

They circled a group of girls jumping rope and came together again, and then Blythe dropped a piece of news that was a real bomb. "You're going to be dance partners with Nathan, aren't you, Lisa? I'll bet you win."

Darci could only stare. Lisa would be dancing with Nathan? Did Lisa really like Nathan? Could Nathan even dance? These were such amazing ideas.

"Oh, Blythe, forget that," Lisa said crossly, and her face reddened as if she wished Blythe hadn't brought it up. Then she added, with a toss of her head, "No, he's already planning to be partners with somebody else."

"Really?" Darci burst out. She was still amazed. Somehow she couldn't believe Nathan would know how to dance. And he already had a partner? Who in the world could that be? "Who is it?" she had to ask.

Lisa shrugged. "I don't know. Who cares? Forget him."

Just then Rebecca went running past them again, and Lisa turned to stare after her. "You know something?" She looked at the group and lowered her voice. "I think I'll put that Weight Watchers folder in her desk."

"Oh, Lisa." Blythe giggled. "Are you really?"

"Yes. I'm going to do it right now before class, and I'll write on it *This means you. Stop eating so many cupcakes!*"

"You mean it?" Jennifer said in an awed voice. "Oh, Lisa!"

"Do you think you should?" Darci asked. "Rebecca ought to lose, sure, but so should lots of people. Going to Weight Watchers would be good and all that, but still, to do that to her . . ."

"Oh, Darci, don't be so chicken," Lisa said sharply. Darci hated being called that. *Chicken?* What was so brave about sneaking a pamphlet into somebody's desk? Darci was just about to point that out when Lisa said, "Here I go." And she rushed off into the crowd ahead of them.

"Do you think she'll actually do it?" Jennifer looked worried.

"Of course she will," Blythe said. "Let's go watch." But Lisa had already disappeared. By the time they reached their room, Lisa was sitting at her desk, busily turning the pages of her notebook. She looked up at them with a little satisfied smile on her face.

Darci sat down at her desk and waited. The rest of the class came crowding into the room. As they all settled into their chairs, Miss Sandor called out, "Too much noise, class."

But Darci was busy watching Rebecca. A rubber band flew into Darci's face from Nathan's direction. But she couldn't look over at him right now. She had to keep her eyes on Rebecca.

Rebecca had finished wiggling around in her seat. She wasn't really any fatter than Blythe and some other kids too. Now Rebecca was raising the lid of her desk. Now she was looking in. Suddenly her head sank lower. She was staring down at something, and Darci could see her cheek, even her ear, turn a dull red. She stayed in that position, half-hidden behind the raised desk top. Then Darci saw the worst of all. A large, shiny tear slid down her face and dropped into the desk. Darci looked across the room toward Lisa and Blythe. They were watching Rebecca with little smirks.

"Class," Miss Sandor called out. "Let's turn around, close your desks, and get ready now."

Darci turned straight in her chair but cast a quick glance toward Rebecca. She was lifting out her notebook, her face flushed, then hunching over her book. Miss Sandor began to talk, but all Darci could think about was that tear —one little drop of water. One person could make that happen to another person. The thought made her insides feel sort of sick. In a way, she'd been in on it too.

Later that afternoon in PE class, Lisa hurried across the playground to Darci. "I couldn't see very well. How did Old Jiggly take it?" she whispered.

"Her face got red—even her ear. And she cried," Darci said.

"Well." Lisa hooked back her hair over her ear and looked around coolly. "Maybe it'll do her some good."

"Seems as if there might be a better way," Darci protested.

"Oh, Darci!" Lisa moved off impatiently. "Someone's got to tell her."

"You don't think she knows?" Darci called after her, but Lisa didn't answer.

That afternoon, the PE teacher, frizzy-haired Miss Sturtz, chose Darci to be one of the team captains for the first time. The other captain was Josie. Darci was pleased to be chosen. And yet as she stood up there and faced everyone, she suddenly knew how hard this was going to be. She almost wished Miss Sturtz had counted off for the teams as she sometimes did. For one thing, Lisa would expect to be picked first. She could see that by Lisa's face already. But instead, Darci chose Jennifer first. When it came her turn again, she took Lisa, then next time, Blythe. Josie had taken Patti, who was always so good at kickball.

"Too bad she got Patti," Lisa whispered.

So they went on with the choosing until there were only a few left. Darci's glance drifted toward Rebecca. If only Josie would choose her. Because now Darci realized what she ought to do, how she could make up for that mean thing Lisa did. But Lisa must have guessed what she was thinking.

"Don't," Lisa whispered. "We don't want her on our team. Make Josie take her."

But Rebecca wasn't that bad at games, and today it would be nice if she weren't picked last. It hurt to hurt someone.

"What's the difference?" Darci whispered back to Lisa.

"Girls," Miss Sturtz called out. "Too much talking."

"Don't." Lisa spit out the word under her breath.

Don't? Why should Lisa say that? Was she the boss around here? Who was captain anyway? Rebecca was staring down at the ground, and Darci knew she must still be sad. Sure, someone always had to wait to the end, but did it have to be Rebecca? Did it have to be today?

Lisa was standing there, pushing back her hair, looking as if she had a right to decide everything, boss everybody.

Something inside Darci stiffened. Chicken, was she? Well, she'd had it with Lisa's orders.

"Rebecca." The word flew out of her mouth like a bird.

Rebecca's head jerked up. Darci could see relief on her face. But as Rebecca walked toward Darci's team, Darci caught a quick glare from Lisa.

After the teams were chosen and they were taking their places, Lisa came rushing over to her and whispered, "Why did you ask her?"

"I felt sorry for her, Lisa," Darci answered.

"But didn't you see how she wouldn't throw that ball to me on the playground? Didn't you feel sorry for me? You shouldn't have done that, Darci." And Lisa ran off.

Darci stared after her for a minute. Lisa was really mad. But now Darci felt angry too. How come Lisa thought she had the right to run everything? Besides, why should Rebecca be nice to her when all Lisa did was stand around and laugh at her?

Once during the game, Jennifer came over and whispered to Darci, "I'm glad you asked Rebecca." Darci nodded gratefully. At least one person liked what she had done. But Darci kept arguing about it in her head during the whole game. She thought about Lisa every time she kicked the ball.

And after the game, Lisa called to Blythe and the others, and they all went off across the playground . . . without Darci.

The Dance Contest

Darci didn't know if Lisa would be friends with her any-more or not. She wasn't sure if she wanted to be friends either. She would miss the others, though, Jennifer espe-cially. Anyway, Lisa was angry. She wouldn't speak to Darci at school, kept calling out to Blythe, Jennifer, and Patti, and hurrying off to the far side of the playground with them. Would Lisa get over her bad mood in a few days or not? And was it really worth it, to have a friend who kept turning against you, who kept wanting to run things just her way?

But Darci was glad she had taken Bo to school. The class as a whole seemed to know her and like her now, and she felt more like a real part of the school. On the bus, the two girls who always sat together moved over and asked her to sit with them and tell them about Bo. It was fun, but it was a bit of a squeeze, three on one seat.

On the day of the dance contest, Darci decided to wear her red skirt, the one that whirled when she spun around. Just in case she got asked. With a white blouse and her brown hair and brown eyes, she thought she looked okay. If she stood far back from the mirror and squinched up her eyes so she could hardly see, she almost looked terrific. She wondered if Lisa and Nathan would be dancing in the contest and Jennifer and the others. Most of all, she wondered if she'd be in it.

Darci walked to the gym that afternoon with Josie and Angela. She stayed with them while the rest of the class gathered there. Lisa was up front with Blythe, watching Miss Sturtz putting a tape into her tape deck. Then Darci spotted Jennifer and Patti across the room, and they waved to her. She waved back, wondering if they had done that because Lisa wasn't with them.

Then Miss Sturtz, who wore a red headband around her frizzy hair today, blew a whistle and called out, "Quiet, please." When everyone stopped talking, she added, "Here are our judges" and introduced an eighth-grade boy and girl. "All right, now," Miss Sturtz continued, "will the dancers please come into the center of the room? The rest of you form a large circle around them."

Miss Sturtz blew the whistle again. Everyone scurried about, getting into the right places, and then Miss Sturtz called out, "Are you ready?"

"Yes," everyone yelled. Some of the boys had said for the last few days they didn't want to watch dancing. They wanted to play their games in PE instead. But now everyone looked interested either in the dancers or in the punch and cookies over on the side table. Darci fell back to the side of the gym, watching to see who would be Lisa's partner. Why should she care about Lisa? She was surprised at herself for hoping Lisa wouldn't be dancing with Nathan.

But Lisa wasn't. Darci saw her join up with tall, blond Wally. And, Darci gasped in surprise, Jennifer was lining up with Bill, Nathan's friend. Who was Nathan dancing with? Darci craned her neck in every direction, trying to spot Nathan. But she didn't see him in the crowd in the middle of the room.

Now Miss Sturtz clapped her hands. "Any more partners for the dance? Come on, last call." Darci felt sad. She wouldn't be in it after all. She'd secretly hoped someone might ask her. Miss Sturtz started a tape, and music hummed and throbbed in the background. The dancers faced each other and began to move to the music. But Nathan wasn't out there either. Of course not. He wouldn't be the type, she was sure. He probably just told Lisa he had plans to dance with someone else so he could get out of it. Her glance moved to Lisa and Wally. Lisa's pale blond hair swung back and forth as she and Wally danced. They looked good, like a matching pair with their blond hair.

Suddenly someone tapped Darci on the shoulder. She whirled around, but there was no one there. "Hah, fooled you," a voice said behind her. She jerked around the other way. There was Nathan grinning at her. She felt silly because he'd tricked her like that. Why was he bugging her anyway?

"Hi," he said, "want to dance?"

"Want to dance?" Did he really say that? Those magic words? The music was loud. Maybe she didn't hear him

right. "What did you say?" she exclaimed. The girls standing next to her giggled.

His dark eyes looked straight at her. "Look," he said. "Your brother says you really know how to dance, better than most. You want to?"

She still felt stunned. Nathan—that incredible pest of a Nathan with the big feet that were always trying to trip her —was asking her to dance? Did he even know how? Was it some kind of a joke? And what about the other girl he was supposed to dance with? Maybe she had turned him down.

Darci wondered if she should say no. But why pass up this chance? So they'd dance the first round. Then they'd be put out, but at least she'd have had a chance to try. "Sure, all right," she said.

"Okay, let's go." Nathan smiled a little. "Wish us luck," he said to the girls on either side of them.

The girls giggled again, and Darci followed Nathan toward the middle of the gym, where almost everyone was dancing now. A few other latecomers were filtering out there too.

Nathan turned to face her. The music was loud, rhythmic but not awfully fast. Just about all the kids were doing a little side step, clapping their hands in time to the music. Darci began to do it too, keeping in step with Nathan. She had a sudden terrible worry. He wouldn't trip her, would he?

"Too bad we don't have Bo here, huh?"

She had to laugh at the thought. "Bo," she exclaimed. "Sure, that's all we need."

"You could pretend to be a snake charmer."

Darci had visions of herself dancing with Bo around her neck and laughed again. Just then, from the corner of her eye, she caught a glimpse of Lisa and Wally. They were doing something better than just stepping and clapping. It looked more like wiggling and shaking. And, uh-oh, now the eighth-grade boy and girl were beginning to go around and tap kids on the shoulder to drop out. She caught a glimpse of Jennifer's anxious face, the glint of her glasses, and hoped Jennifer wouldn't be put out yet. But how about herself? She didn't want to be put out either. This was fun, even if it was with Nathan. She began to do an extra little step that just fit in with the beat. To her surprise, Nathan did it too.

Nathan grinned. "Try this," he said. He whirled around, then came back to meet her face-to-face again. "Ready? Let's do it together."

Darci spun around, feeling her red skirt whirl out nicely, and came back to meet Nathan again. His dark eyes looked pleased. "Great," he said. "They can't put us out, right?"

Darci felt astounded. Nathan, she could see already, could stay in touch with the rhythm, better than Rick, actually. And Nathan seemed to want to keep on dancing with her. She relaxed some. She didn't think he would try to trip her, after all.

"I heard you were planning to dance with somebody else. That's what Lisa said."

"Yes, well, sure . . ." He smiled at her suddenly. "It was you."

"Me!" She was startled. He'd planned it all along? She felt warm, pleased. "You seem to know a lot about dancing."

"My dad made me go to dancing school. It wasn't too bad."

They began to dance faster to keep up with the music. Faces slid past her eyes. Some she knew—Josie, Angela, her dark hair flying. Jennifer again, Anne's red hair, and Lisa, suddenly looking over at her, then coming closer. She leaned to say in Darci's ear, "Don't fall down, Darci" in a mocking voice. "I mean, anyone who could fall off a horse . . ."

Lisa broke away, smiling smugly. And for a moment, Darci had a dizzy feeling. What if she did fall right here in the gym? What a terrible idea. Was the floor tilting? Oh, crazy idea. Forget it, forget that Lisa. Darci looked at Nathan and wondered if he'd heard what Lisa said.

The judges were walking around again. Darci danced faster to keep up with Nathan and, hurray, the judges passed them by. She glanced around and saw the crowd had thinned out a lot.

"We're really hanging in there." Nathan smiled at her. And they jiggled and swayed to the music, facing each other. Luckily it wasn't that close kind of dancing where they had to hang on to each other and worry about sweaty hands and bad breath and all that. But this way was fun, so much fun. The rhythm and the beat seemed to sweep through her and helped her know just what to do.

But the judges were at it again, tapping more shoulders, and all of a sudden there were only four couples left. The circle of onlookers pressed around them. Darci was amazed. Was there any chance she and Nathan might win?

"Oh, man," Nathan exclaimed. "Look at us, Darci. We're still here. Let's do this." Snapping his fingers, he bent his knees, crouching lower and lower. She did the same. They were stooping way down, laughing at each other. "Now, spring up and twirl around," Nathan said.

They did it in unison. Darci felt her red skirt flying and heard, unbelievably, clapping from the other students.

That Nathan was so good. And maybe she was doing okay too.

But now the judges were circling again. Oh, what was going on? Two more couples were being asked to stop. Amazing! Lisa and Wally would be the only other couple left. How could this be happening? How could it be narrowed down to just the two of them, the two of them who weren't friends anymore? She stared at Nathan in amazement, then over at Lisa in a moment of worry.

"Let's win it," Nathan whispered, his face glowing. "Let's do this again." He crouched down. She did too. This was so much fun. They leaped up, snapping their fingers. Nathan wanted to win, and besides, so did she.

Darci glanced over at Lisa and Wally again, their blond heads swaying. They looked so good they would probably win. But it was fun anyway.

Darci whirled and clapped her hands. Ah-h-h, it was great. Her feet felt light and airy and seemed to know just what to do.

But now the judges were heading toward Lisa and Wally. How incredible! And maybe that was why Wally suddenly threw himself backward on the floor and began to do break dancing that she had seen the guys do in the mall and sometimes here at school. The judges said something to Lisa and then . . . and then they came over to Nathan and Darci! To Darci's amazement, she heard them say over the music, "You two are the winners of the dance contest."

"No kidding!" Nathan beamed. "We won, Darci!"

But Wally kept on whirling around on his shoulders down on the floor. Maybe he didn't know he'd lost. Suddenly he clutched his mouth and winced in pain. And he

93

struggled to his feet. Blood dripped from his mouth. Everyone crowded around him.

Miss Sturtz ran and got some ice cubes from the punch bowl, and in a few minutes the bleeding had stopped. His lip, where he'd bitten it, was all puffy, but he was okay.

And then a lot of kids gathered around Darci and Nathan and said, "Great, you were terrific," "Way to go," "Really awesome, you two," and all that. And Miss Sturtz gave Nathan and Darci each a new record. It was all so exciting, so unbelievable. The only trouble was, afterward Lisa told everybody that she and Wally were just about to win first place. But, of course, Wally had to go and bite his lip, so the judges gave first place to Nathan and Darci. And besides, everyone knew that new kids always get special favors.

But Darci tried not to think about Lisa as she climbed on the bus after school. One thing she felt sure about, Lisa would not want to be friends, now that Darci had beaten her in the dance contest. But Darci wasn't going to worry about friends right now. She kept telling herself how lucky and happy she was to win a dance contest. It was really terrific, wasn't it?

Finding the Frisbee

Darci hurried home, eager to tell her mom the news. But when she opened the front door, there was a note on the hall table from Mom saying she had taken Donny over to a boy's house to play. So even Donny had a friend. Darci tried not to feel a little twinge of sadness, of envy. It was good for Donny and way better than having him hanging around all the time, bugging everybody.

Then she noticed a letter from Luanne on the hall table. Oh, how great! At last. Darci seized the letter and rushed up to her room. No need to look under her bed anymore, thank heavens, now that Bo was safely back in his cage.

Her room looked sort of nice and cozy with its sloping ceiling and flowery old wallpaper and warm sunshine streaming through the windows. It could be fun here if only . . . She flopped down on the bed and tore open the letter. How great it was going to be to hear what Luanne had to say, and wait till she wrote to Luanne and told her all about the dance contest.

Luanne wrote all about a trip to Disneyland last Saturday; how a kid was caught in the cafeteria for stealing a piece of cake; how a friend's house was used for a TV show; about a sleep-over at a friend's house for her birthday. But all this was strange. It all seemed so far away now. It didn't have anything to do with Darci anymore. She didn't feel like part of it. Then Luanne wrote *I'm glad you're having so much fun in Oakwood and you've got new friends. That must have been fantastic when you caught the snake. A lot of people say you're lucky to move there. But I miss you, Darci. Write back soon. Your friend, Luanne.*

That made Darci sad. She missed Luanne too. Sure, she'd won a dance contest, and she'd given a good snake talk, and been surprised by Nathan being so nice to her! She'd never get over that. But it still wasn't the same as having a friend. There was still that lonely feeling. And it had hurt to have Lisa turn against her. Well, she'd write to Luanne right now. She settled down at her desk.

Sometime later, she heard boys' voices out front. It sounded like Nathan and Bill. She got up and went over to the window to watch them. They were out in the street, tossing a Frisbee back and forth. She watched Nathan reach up to catch it, his curly black hair flung back as he leaped off the ground and snapped the Frisbee out of the air. He was definitely sort of cute. And it had been so much fun to dance with him. What a surprise, to find out how good a dancer he was and that he wanted to dance with her. Was it possible that he liked her?

96

Suddenly he glanced up toward her window and motioned to her to come on out. Well, why not? Maybe she would. Maybe she liked him. She ran downstairs and out the front door to the street.

"Here, catch, Darci the dancer!" Nathan hurled the Frisbee toward her with a grin.

"You're the one." She laughed as she caught the red Frisbee and flung it back to him. "Wasn't he good?" she called over to Bill. Even from here, she could see the pleased look on Nathan's face.

"Sure." Bill's freckled face looked admiring. "But it takes two to win, you know."

That was nice of Bill. She was glad he'd danced with Jennifer. They kept tossing the Frisbee back and forth to one another. It was fun, playing with the guys, and they didn't seem to mind.

Pretty soon, her mom and Donny and Dad and Rick all came driving up the street in Mom's old station wagon. Mom had picked up Dad at the train station, as usual. Dad sometimes rode the commuter train into the city. How surprised they were going to be when they heard about the dance contest. Darci smiled a little to herself. Dad would be really impressed.

It was beginning to get late, and soon they would have to go in. After a bit, Bill said, "I have to go home. See you guys later." He went over to the curb and picked up his bike and started off down the street.

"Good-bye, Bill," Darci called. "I better be going in a minute too," she added to Nathan.

"Here, one more catch." Nathan threw her the Frisbee once more, but it went high in the air. "Jump!" he yelled.

She leaped into the air, but it was too high. It kept on curving over her head and landed in the big bushes along the front of her house. Darci started for the bushes. It was quite dark now and hard to see. She began to poke around in there. Suddenly, there was Nathan beside her. "Here, I'll help you look for it, Darci."

They pushed through the bushes together. "There it is." Darci bent to pick it up, but suddenly she realized they were all by themselves, just the two of them, close together in the leafy bushes. Bill had gone.

Nathan had been so nice to her today. It made her think of something she had been wanting to say to him. "Nathan," she said, "about that time on TV. I really was sorry." She could try to blame it on Lisa too. Still, Lisa wasn't the one who got him in trouble.

"Aw, that's okay, Darci. I knew you were. Besides, I shouldn't have made that face."

So there was no need to say anything more, was there? And besides, just then Nathan reached out and touched her arm.

"Darci," he said, "let's . . . let's kiss." She looked at him, startled. In the half-light, she could see him coming closer. "Come on." Now he had his arms around her.

"Well—"

She held her face toward him, and then they kissed. What hot lips he had! But it didn't feel too bad.

Then with a terrific rustling of the bushes, he leaped out of there, and she jumped out too. "Good-bye, Nathan. See you tomorrow." He darted off into the darkness toward his house, and she toward hers.

A kiss! She touched her lips as she reached for the front door. Did a kiss show? Nathan. She had to smile a little. She wondered if her parents would notice anything different.

She flung open the front door, hoping Rick or Donny

wouldn't say, "Where've you been, what took you—" and things like that. But instead, Rick called out, "Hey, Darci, Jennifer phoned. She wants you to come over Friday for a sleep-over."

Darci could hardly believe it. "Are you sure?"

"Yeah, yeah. Some other girl—Patti—is coming too."

She beamed. Someone, a friend, wanted her to come spend the night. Jennifer! That nice Jennifer was going to be her friend.

But as she stepped inside, she saw Rick and Donny and her mother and father all down on their hands and knees on the living-room floor. Her parents were looking under the couch. Donny was poking under the green chair, and Rick was peering into the fireplace.

"Oh, no!" Darci exclaimed. "I don't believe it. Bo must have escaped from his cage again!"

About the Author

MARTHA TOLLES wrote about a dance contest, she says, because "I know just how much fun dancing is, having done a lot of it myself." But especially, she says, "I wanted to write about one of life's biggest needs, the need for friends."

A graduate of Smith College, Mrs. Tolles is also the author of *Katie and Those Boys, Katie for President, Katie's Baby-sitting Job,* and *Who's Reading Darci's Diary?* She and her attorney husband, the parents of six children, live in San Marino, California.

Delicious New Apples®

Exciting Series for You!

ANIMAL INN™ by Virginia Vail

When 13-year-old Val Taylor comes home from school, she spends her afternoons with a menagerie of horses, dogs, and cats—the residents of Animal Inn, her dad's veterinary clinic.

PETS ARE FOR KEEPS #1   **$2.50 / $3.50 Can.**

A KID'S BEST FRIEND #2   **$2.50 / $3.50 Can.**

MONKEY BUSINESS #3   **$2.50 / $3.50 Can.**

THE BABY-SITTERS CLUB™ by Ann M. Martin

Meet Kristy, Claudia, Mary Anne, and Stacey...the four members of the Baby-sitters Club! They're 7th graders who get involved in all kinds of adventures—with school, boys, and, of course, baby-sitting!

FREE
Baby-sitters Kit!
Details in Books 1, 2, and 3

KRISTY'S GREAT IDEA #1   **$2.50 / $3.50 Can.**

CLAUDIA AND THE PHANTOM PHONE CALLS #2 **$2.50 / $3.50 Can.**

THE TRUTH ABOUT STACEY #3   **$2.50 / $3.50 Can.**

MARY ANNE SAVES THE DAY #4   **$2.50 / $3.50 Can.**

APPLE® CLASSICS

Kids everywhere have loved these stories for a long time...and so will you!

THE CALL OF THE WILD by Jack London
After being stolen from his home, Buck—part St. Bernard, part German Shepherd—returns to the wild...as the leader of a wolf pack!   **$2.50 / $3.95 Can.**

LITTLE WOMEN by Louisa May Alcott (abridged)
The March sisters were more than just sisters—they were friends! You'll never forget Meg, Jo, Beth, and Amy.   **$2.50 / $3.95 Can.**

WHITE FANG by Jack London
White Fang—half dog, half wolf—is captured by the Indians, tortured by a cowardly man, and he becomes a fierce, deadly fighter. Will he ever find a loving master?
$2.50 / $3.50 Can.

Look in your bookstores now for these great titles!

📖 **Scholastic Books**   APP871

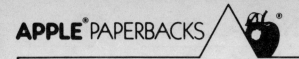
APPLE® PAPERBACKS

Delicious Reading!

NEW APPLE® TITLES $2.50 each

☐ FM 40382-6 **Oh Honestly, Angela!** Nancy K. Robinson
☐ FM 40305-2 **Veronica the Show-Off** Nancy K. Robinson
☐ FM 33662-2 **DeDe Takes Charge!** Johanna Hurwitz
☐ FM 40180-7 **Sixth Grade Can Really Kill You** Barthe DeClements
☐ FM 40874-7 **Stage Fright** Ann M. Martin
☐ FM 40513-6 **Witch Lady Mystery** Carol Beach York
☐ FM 40452-0 **Ghosts Who Went to School** Judith Spearing
☐ FM 33946-X **Swimmer** Harriet May Savitz
☐ FM 40406-7 **Underdog** Marilyn Sachs

BEST-SELLING APPLE® TITLES

☐ FM 40725-2 **Nothing's Fair in Fifth Grade** Barthe DeClements
☐ FM 40466-0 **The Cybil War** Betsy Byars
☐ FM 40529-2 **Amy and Laura** Marilyn Sachs
☐ FM 40950-6 **The Girl with the Silver Eyes** Willo Davis Roberts
☐ FM 40755-4 **Ghosts Beneath Our Feet** Betty Ren Wright
☐ FM 40605-1 **Help! I'm a Prisoner in the Library** Eth Clifford
☐ FM 40724-4 **Katie's Baby-sitting Job** Martha Tolles
☐ FM 40607-8 **Secrets in the Attic** Carol Beach York
☐ FM 40534-9 **This Can't Be Happening at Macdonald Hall!**
              Gordon Korman
☐ FM 40687-6 **Just Tell Me When We're Dead!** Eth Clifford

📕 **Scholastic Inc. P.O. Box 7502, 2932 E. McCarty Street, Jefferson City, MO 65102**

Please send me the books I have checked above. I am enclosing $_____
(please add $1.00 to cover shipping and handling). Send check or money order-no cash or C.O.D.'s please.

Name_____

Address_____

City_____State/Zip_____
Please allow four to six weeks for delivery. Offer good in U.S.A. only. Sorry, mail order not available to residents of Canada.

APP872

Bring home
SLEEPOVER FRIENDS!™

Here's an exciting excerpt from *PATTI'S LUCK #1*, coming in August:

Patti arranged her hair into a row of purple spikes, sort of like the Statue of Liberty's crown. Stephanie's purple curls stuck straight out, as though she'd had an electric shock.

Kate was reading the label on the jar of styling gel. "This stuff stains cloth," she said. "We'd better wash it out before it gets on anything."

Patti went into the bathroom. But she was out in a second.

"No hot water? Let it run for a minute or two," Stephanie told her.

Patti shook her purple head. "No," she said. "There's *no water at all*."

The water main hadn't been repaired when we started home the next morning. Our purple hair was standing straight up.

Donald Foster was in his front yard, fiddling with a lawn mower. "Looking good, girls! Where are your broomsticks?"

Broomsticks, bad luck, witches. . . . After all that happened at the sleepover, I couldn't help thinking of . . . the *Beekman curse*. What if Kate's words were right, and the time was right, and the moon and the stars were in the right places?

Truth or dare, scary movies, all-night boy talk—they're all part of SLEEPOVER FRIENDS.

Watch for back-of-the-book information on how *you* can get the official SLEEPOVER FRIENDS Sleepover Kit—everything you need to know to have a great sleepover party!

Coming in August... PATTI'S LUCK Sleepover Friends #1
by Susan Saunders $2.50/$3.50 Can.

◖◗ Scholastic Books

SLE872